X

WITHDRAWN

D0349512

TWO FOR TANNER

TWO FOR TANNER

Lawrence Block

BOURNEMOUTH

- — 1999

LIBRARIES

CHIVERS LARGE PRINT
BATH

British Library Cataloguing in Publication Data available

This Large Print edition published by Chivers Press, Bath, 1999.

Published by arrangement with Oldcastle Books Ltd.

U.K. Hardcover ISBN 0 7540 3657 X
U.K. Softcover   ISBN 0 7540 3658 8

The right of Lawrence Block to be identified as the author of this work has been asserted by him in accordance with the Copyright, Designs and Patents Act 1988.

All rights reserved.

Printed and bound in Great Britain by
Redwood Books, Trowbridge, Wiltshire

CHAPTER ONE

It wasn't a cell exactly. Not in the usual sense of the word. When one speaks of a prison cell, one implies rather a sort of room in a sort of building, with perhaps a barred door and window. A stone or cement floor. A cot, a dangling light bulb, a pot of some sort in which various bodily functions may be performed.

I had been in such a cell once, in Istanbul. I hadn't liked it much, but at least it was a genuine and proper prison cell.

Not like my current home. Not like this idiot contrivance in which I was presently trapped, a rude box eight feet square and four feet high, constructed entirely of bamboo, and suspended from the limb of a tall tree, with its bottom about five feet from the ground.

You couldn't call it a cell, then. What you could call it, if you were inclined to call it anything, was a large birdcage. And it was the only sort of birdcage to be found for miles around. Birds are not caged in dense teak forests far in the north of Thailand. There are plenty of birds to be found, bright of plumage and swift of flight and shrill of voice, screeching hellishly in the tops of tall trees. Such birds are not overly fond of captivity.

But, then, neither was I.

I had been in the cage ever since the

1

guerrilla patrol captured me four days previously. It was almost impossible to believe that only four days had passed, but one must rely on the evidence of one's senses; the sun had risen and set four times, and that had to have some significance.

But I had never lived through longer days. The endless quality of those hours was in part a function of the particular design of my bamboo cage, which seemed to have been devised as a special form of Oriental torture. One could not stand up. One could crouch, and there was barely enough headroom to sort of crawl around, but crawling didn't really work. A single rope fastened to the center of the cage's top was all that connected my cage to a tree limb far overhead. Thus, if one moved from the very middle of the cage, the thing tilted—at which point one was unceremoniously pitched forward to the juncture of floor and wall.

Even if this had not been so, there was little enough reason to move from one part of the cage to the next, since one section of it was very much like another. True, I could just manage to peer through the bamboo sides at the guerrilla encampment surrounding me. I did this, at one time or another, from every side of the cage. I saw, at one time or another, any number of huts, cooking fires, rifles, machetes, sharpened stakes, and Siamese guerrillas. I saw various articles of my

2

clothing—I was quite naked in my cage, like a bird plucked free of feathers—being worn by various guerrillas. I saw nothing, however, that was sufficiently deserving of a second glance to tempt me to risk leaving the point of balance in the center of the cage.

There was a small hole in the center of the floor, a small square hole cleverly cut into the bamboo flooring, through which a bowl of wormy rice was passed to me twice a day if they remembered and less frequently if they did not. Now and then someone would also pass me a cup of greasy water, and now and then I would void whatever had to be voided through the same aperture. One would have thought that with so little food and water coming into the cage, a correspondingly small quantity of matter would have to leave it. But there must have been something corrupt in either the rice or the water or both, some sociable amoebas bent on causing amoebic dysentery. Around the middle of the third day I began to worry that, eating so little and voiding so much, I was in danger of disappearing entirely or of turning myself inside out. But by the fourth day the dysentery went away; I guess I had starved it to death.

I couldn't stand up, I couldn't walk around, I couldn't rest, I couldn't eat properly. I stayed in one spot, now squatting on my haunches, now stretched out on my back, now with my legs knotted into the Yoga lotus posture. I

3

grew increasingly hot, hungry, bored, and uncomfortable with the passage of time. At the beginning I had been afraid they would kill me. Now I was beginning to fear that they wouldn't.

It might not have been so bad if I could have slept. But when I was eighteen years old, a piece of North Korean shrapnel had been rudely deposited in my brain, and in the course of this, something called my sleep center had been destroyed. Medical science is not entirely certain what the sleep center is or what it does. Mine isn't, and whatever it once did, it no longer does; consequently I have not slept in seventeen years.

All in all, I've found this more an advantage than not. In addition to bringing me a $112 government disability check every month, my insomnia leaves me with that many more hours per day to get things done, obviates the necessity for hotel rooms while traveling, and otherwise enhances life.

But sleep, in addition to being sore labor's bath, healer of life's wounds, the death of each day's life, and all the other things Macbeth called it, is also a handy time-waster to ease one through stretches of excruciating boredom. My trek through the jungle had been sufficiently exhausting to tire me considerably, and but for that shred of shrapnel, I would probably have spent half my caged hours in blissful unconsciousness.

4

Instead I stayed awake.

I have never had so little to do. During the first day I tried to attract attention by making noise. I called out now and then in Siamese, which I speak moderately well, and in Khmer, which I don't. No one ever went so far as to answer me, but I found that whenever I made any noise, someone came over and raised one side of the cage, thus sending me sprawling over to the other side. After each utterance of mine, regardless of pitch or language or content, had been similarly rewarded, I learned my lesson. I stopped talking.

And no one talked to me. My silence was met by silence, with no interrogation whatsoever. I had decided at first to try convincing them that I was not an American agent named Evan Michael Tanner and then I decided to convince them that I was. Both of these decisions were quite irrelevant. No one asked me anything, not name or rank or serial number, nothing at all. I stayed where I was and waited for something to happen, but it didn't.

I don't know what I was waiting for anyway. Divine intercession perhaps. A bolt of lightning could strike the tree, thus causing my cage to drop to the ground and shatter itself apart. The encampment could be raided by troops loyal to His Majesty's Government. Or by the Marines. Or the U.S. Horse Cavalry. Most of the time, though, I tried to avoid

5

thinking about what it was that I awaited. Since there was nothing to do in the cage and no way to get out of the cage and no escape route if I did get out, waiting was almost an end in itself; I didn't have to wait *for* anything.

Until late one afternoon someone finally spoke to me. A hand poked a rice bowl through the central hole in the bottom of the cage. I snatched the bowl rather greedily—they had, by accident or on purpose, missed my morning feeding. I wolfed down the rice, worms and all. This sounds even worse than it was; after you've done it once or twice, worms cease to turn your stomach, and protein, after all, is protein. I sent the bowl back empty, received a cup of tepid water in return, drank the water, returned the cup, and a soft, sad voice said, 'Tomorrow.'

Or perhaps the voice said, 'Morning.' Siamese, like so many other languages, makes no distinction between the two concepts. Whether my new friend meant tomorrow generally or tomorrow morning in particular was indeterminable from the single word spoken.

So I said, 'Tomorrow?' Or 'Morning?' In any case I repeated the word he had said.

'Upon the rising of the sun.' Well, that cleared things up.

'What will happen then?'

'Upon the rising of the sun,' he said mournfully, 'they will kill you.'

6

His words filled me with hope.

Not, let me add, because I thought he was right and hoped for death as a respite from life in a cage. Uncomfortable as my bamboo home might be, the alternative he proposed seemed even less desirable. The cause for hope stemmed not from the information I had received but from the way the message had been couched. It was not what he said but how he said it.

Consider: not *We will kill you* but *They will kill you*. Thus implicitly disassociating himself from any personal involvement in the act, either active or passive. And his tone of voice accentuated this—*they* were going to kill me, and *he* was sad about it. It even seemed likely that he had violated orders by giving me this bit of news.

'They will kill you at sunrise,' he said again.

I had been sitting in the lotus posture, legs folded up so that each foot rested on top of the opposite knee. I unknotted my legs, stretched out, rolled over onto my stomach, and put my mouth to the aperture in the cage bottom. The cage tilted slightly, but I remained fairly well balanced, physically if not emotionally. And I was able to see my informant clearly in the twilight. He was in his late teens, short and slender, with neatly cropped glossy black hair, and the clean, doll-like features prevalent throughout that part of the world.

7

'There was talk of getting you a woman,' he went on mournfully. 'Usually when a man is condemned to die, he is first given a woman. It is the custom. Formerly it was done only for men who had fathered no children of their own, so that they might have a final opportunity to perpetuate their seed. But then it was said that no man can ever be certain that he has sired children, and so it was decided that every condemned man should spend the night before his execution with a woman.'

Imminent death is supposed to have an aphrodisiacal effect. It certainly didn't this time. I didn't want a woman. I didn't even want a good meal or a glass of whiskey. All I really wanted was to get the hell out of the cage.

'But,' he continued, 'there will not be a woman for you. It was decided that you are a capitalist imperialist dog and a white devil, and that your seed must not be mingled with the love juices of our women. It is what they decided.'

They again. I started to say how good it was of him to tell me, but he was not interested in such pap. He had more important things on his mind, and I was in every sense a captive audience.

'I have never had a woman,' he said.

'Never?'

'Never in all my days. I have, however, spent many hours thinking about such a thing.'

8

'I can imagine.'

'I look at the women,' he said dreamily. 'I watch them walking, you know, the shapes of their bodies, the legs, the tilt of their heads, the tinkling sounds of their voices. Like little brass bells. I think about them a great deal.' He fell momentarily silent, perhaps to think about them some more. His brown eyes were very large, and beads of sweat formed on his smooth forehead. 'There are times,' he said suddenly, 'when I can honestly think of nothing else.'

'And you have never had one.'

'Never.'

I felt like the *Playboy* Advisor. 'Well, why don't you, uh, go and get one?'

'How?'

'Well—'

'Women do not like me,' he said. 'And when I am near one of them, I become nervous, my hands sweat, and my mouth goes dry, a dryness in the back of my mouth and in my throat, and words die in my mouth like fish flapping themselves to death upon the shore, and my knees turn to water, and my head spins . . .'

He certainly had a problem. Under less restricted circumstances I probably would have been a good deal more sympathetic. But I too had a problem, and mine had a temporal urgency his did not share. Another few hours of celibacy would not kill him, while a few more hours in my birdcage would resolve itself

9

in hanging or decapitation or whatever sort of fun and games was on the morrow's agenda.

'I suppose you have had women?'

'Oh,' I said. 'Yes, uh, yes I have.' And so I had, and it was the possession of one such, Tuppence Ngawa by name, that had brought me to Thailand in the first place.

'Many women?'

'Not too many.'

'What are they like?'

'Better than ham.'

'Pardon me?'

'Never mind,' I said. It was a reference to an old joke about a priest and a rabbi, a joke that couldn't make much sense to a Thai. Besides, it was a diversion; the main thing now was to find a way to escape, and the only hope was this unhappy virgin, and—

Of course.

'There is nothing on earth to match the embrace of a woman,' I said. 'I am not without extensive experience in such matters and I can tell you that no other sensation is its equivalent. The soft, sweet texture of female flesh, of breasts and legs, of hungry lips and tender doe-like eyes, the taste of a woman, the subtle but pungent aroma of a woman . . .'

I went on in this vein for quite a while. It had the desired effect. The poor clown had a fairly short fuse to begin with, and this was sheer agony for him. 'Stop,' he said at last. 'Please stop.'

'It is unfair that you have never known such joy. If only I were free, I would do something about it.'

'You would?'

'Of course, my friend.'

'But what would you do?'

'I would help you find a woman.'

'You could do this?'

'With ease and with pleasure.'

He hesitated for a moment. 'It is a trick,' he said suddenly. 'It is a capitalist imperialist trick, a trick.'

And he went away.

I slapped a mosquito and said something obscene in Siamese. At sunrise they were going to kill me. I didn't know how and I didn't know why, but it hardly mattered. I had to get away, and they were not going to let me get away, and my little virginal friend had decided that he did not trust me. I hadn't slept in seventeen years and tomorrow I would go to sleep and I would never wake up. I could barely remember what sleep was like, but the way I remembered it, the best part of it was waking up refreshed, and that was a part I couldn't look forward to. They were going to put me to sleep, and that would be the end of it.

'You would really get me a woman?'

He had returned. It was darker now, and his voice was more urgent now, and I could guess what he had been spending his time thinking about. Capitalist imperialist trick or no, I was his one chance, just as he was mine. Alliances have been forged upon less than that.

'I will.'

'I have decided to trust you, my friend.'

'Good.'

'I shall help you.'

'*They* will kill me at sunrise unless *we* do something about it.'

'We will escape.'

'Good.'

'Together.'

'Good.'

'I go now. When it is darker, when the camp sleeps, I shall return. I go now, my friend, my good friend.'

I celebrated by slapping another mosquito. They were fairly bad during the days and considerably worse at night, and night was coming. The mosquitoes had bothered me most the first day in the jungle, but by the time I was captured the ferocity of their attack had diminished to a great extent. By now they mostly let me alone. What with my diet and my dysentery and the raids of earlier mosquitoes, I must have been running out of blood.

I wondered if my little friend would ever come back and whether his help would make much difference one way or the other. The cage could only be opened by lowering it to the ground, which in turn could not be done without making a hell of a racket and waking the entire camp. Furthermore, sentries stayed awake the entire night, so that even if I escaped from the cage, I would probably be caught trying to sneak out of the camp. And if I wasn't caught, I would have a whole jungle to walk through.

I wondered if the Land Rover still worked. It had been at about the end of its tether anyway; the path that had brought me the last little bit of the way to the guerrilla encampment was barely wide enough to admit the car, and was so overgrown in spots that a less rugged vehicle would have given up miles earlier. So even if the Land Rover were still operable, which was doubtful, I couldn't count on it to take me anywhere.

Was there anything of value in the car? Nothing much, really. The extra clothing I had brought would have been appropriated by the guerrillas, just as they had taken what I was wearing. They probably would have left the butterfly-collecting equipment alone. The spreading board, the killing jar, the butterfly net, all the little accoutrements designed to cover my presence in the jungles and rubber plantations of Thailand, and all quite wasted now. These guerrillas did not seem to care whether I was a bona fide lepidopterist or a sneaky spy. All they wanted to do was kill me.

I closed my eyes and cursed. I cursed Tuppence's father for going back to Africa and conceiving Tuppence in the first place. I cursed Tuppence for coming first from Nairobi to New York, and then from New York to Bangkok. I cursed the King of Thailand for being a modern jazz enthusiast and I cursed Tuppence for being a thief, and over and above it all I cursed myself for being several different kinds of a damned fool.

Then I stopped cursing and started thinking, and of the two thinking turned out to be the more productive, because by the time night had fallen once and for all and my little Thai friend had crept soundlessly to my cage and whispered his presence, I had it all figured out.

'The automobile,' I said. 'Is it still where I left it?'

'The automobile?'

'The motor car.'

'The motor car?'

'The automobile, the motor car, the horse of metal with rubber feet—'

'Ah, the automobile! It is on the path in the clearing to the south.'

'And has anything been taken from it?'

'Your clothing was taken, and the rubber feet were removed.'

I wondered why. 'But the other objects in the back seat?'

'They are where they were.'

'And could you gain access to the automobile?'

'I could.'

'And bring me certain articles from the back

14

seat?'

'I could.'

'Then, I think we may have a chance for freedom. You will have many tasks to perform between now and the rising of the sun, but if you work very hard and if luck is with us, I think there is a fair chance that we may succeed.'

'And I will have a woman?'

'You will have a woman.'

'Then, it is worth whatever risks must be taken.'

'It certainly is.'

'And you will be saved, and we will run away, and they will not lead you to the chopping block and sever your head by driving the blade of the ax through your neck.'

I swallowed. 'Is that what they had planned?'

'It is how executions are performed here.'

'A sort of neck-Thai party,' I said. But I said it in English because of course it wouldn't work in Siamese, and in English it made no sense to my little friend. 'An old saying of my forefathers,' I explained. 'Nothing at all. We need not concern ourselves with it. We have much work ahead of us.'

'Tell me what I must do.'

'Go to the automobile and remove the battery—'

'What is a battery?'

'You raise the hood and—'

'The hood?'

'We have much work ahead of us,' I said.

CHAPTER TWO

My first meeting with Miss T'pani Ngawa took place at a PAUL meeting held on a rainy Thursday night in a storefront church on Lenox Avenue at 138th Street. I lived several blocks and a few light-years away on 107th Street near Broadway, and so I walked to the meeting through the cold, impartial rain, which fell alike on black and white, and through the cries of *Hey, Whitey!* and *What you doin' up here, Mr. Charlie?*

PAUL is the Pan-African Unity League, and what I was doin' up there, Mr. Charlie, was going to a meeting of it. The climate at the meeting itself was drier and warmer in every respect. There was a brief report on the slaughter of Ibos in Nigeria, a somewhat more extended lecture on conditions in the Congo, and, finally, a report by Miss Ngawa on social and economic progress in Kenya.

When the meeting ended, she and I went out for coffee. We had an immediate common bond. I was the only Caucasian at the meeting, and she was the only African. All the others in attendance were American Negroes.

'The Back-To-Africa bit,' she said. 'Bwana

16

and simba and the bloody drums in the bloody jungle. Shee-it, baby, like it is all something else, you dig?'

As a man is, so does he speak. Tuppence, being a highly unorthodox combination of things, spoke an English all her own. She was the only child of a Kenyan mother and an American father. Her father, one Willie Jackson, had been a follower of Marcus Garvey and an African Nationalist. The Army sent him to North Africa during the Second World War, where he rather promptly deserted and headed south. He changed his name to Willie Ngawa, married Tuppence's mother, and conceived Tuppence.

Later, during the Mau Mau uprising, Willie Ngawa was sentenced to death for miscegenation. Like most American Negroes, he had a certain amount of Caucasian blood in his veins and arteries and capillaries; thus an extremist wing of the Mau Mau felt that it was criminal for him to marry a full-blooded Negress. He was accordingly taken from his hut one night when Tuppence was very small and he was bound hand and foot and carried off into the jungle, where his captors broke both his arms and legs and introduced a regiment of army ants into his rectum. The ants promptly began to devour Willie Ngawa's bowels, somewhere in the course of which Willie Ngawa had the good sense to expire.

Tuppence and her mother subsequently

moved to Nairobi and lived in that city while Kenya transformed itself from British Crown Colony to independent republic. She grew up learning English and Swahili and sang the folk songs of Kenya. She went to college in London, began singing with a jazz group there, and ultimately came to New York, where she took an apartment on the Lower East Side, got a more or less steady gig with a local jazz quartet, and concurrently developed a reputation as an African folk singer at Harlem rent parties and East Village loft sessions.

Her speech reflected all of these influences. The prevailing accent was upper-class English, spoken with the special precision that the language receives only when it issues from the lips of a citizen of one of the Commonwealth countries. No Englishman ever born speaks as pure a strain of English as a well-educated Kenyan or Pakistani or Nigerian. Intermingled with this accent was a strong undercurrent of Harlem diction liberally salted with bop slang and peppered with bits and pieces of Swahili. The result was as profoundly individualistic a speech pattern as I have ever heard, singularly Tuppence.

I received Tuppence's history a little at a time over a period of several hours after leaving the PAUL meeting. We drank several cups of coffee in a chrome-and-formica diner on 125th Street, ate sweet and pungent almond duck at the Great Shanghai, and

18

wound up, happily enough, at my apartment on 107th Street. We sat on my couch drinking a Yugoslav white wine, which, though not particularly good, is not particularly bad either, and which is extremely cheap; the recent devaluation of the dinar had brought the price down to around 79c a bottle. We finished one bottle and got most of the way through a second, by which time we were assuring each other that the wine was really very good after all, wasn't it, and that it seemed to improve with each glass.

And then Tuppence said, 'You dig this li'l pickaninny, Bwana Evan? Do you now?'

'Ah, the natives are restless.'

'They are indeed. Do you think you might extinguish that barbaric cacophony'—we had been listening to a Miles Davis record—'and put on something tribal?'

I made sure Minna's door was closed. Minna was a seven-year-old Lithuanian girl who had moved into my apartment several months previously, and who seemed likely to stay forever. She was sleeping soundly, and I closed her door and changed the jazz record for a Folk-ways recording of Kenyan and Ugandan chants, dances, and work songs. I turned the volume down low, and Tuppence bounced off the couch and turned the volume up high, and laughed gaily and kicked off her shoes and began to dance.

'Native girl dance for you, Bwana Evan.'

Her white eyes rolled in her dark face. 'Native girl make you hot with passion, wild with lust. Native girl turn you on, baby. You better believe it.'

I don't know whether or not her dance was an authentic example of Kenyan tribal folk-dancing. I rather think not. It seemed a combination of African dance and current American styles, with the limbs loose, the hips shaking, the buttocks twitching, and the whole body transfigured by an endless chaotic rhythm. And through it all Tuppence's lips showed a smile of eternal female knowledge, and her huge eyes twinkled in calculated abandon.

She was a striking girl. She was the wrong color to win a Miss America contest, the shade of good, well-rubbed walnut. She was tall and long-legged, with a high, protruding bottom and a flat stomach and full breasts. Her face was long, oval in shape, with a high, broad forehead and a cap of tight, kinky black curls.

So she danced, and we looked at each other, and something that had started building at the PAUL meeting clicked neatly and finally into place, and we both knew that the evening was going to end properly. Because the special magic was there. It is not often present, and without it there is really no reason on earth why a man and woman should bother having anything to do with one another. But when it is there, it is a very welcome thing indeed. It was there now, for both of us, and we both knew it and we both seemed happy.

'This step shows that the villagers are rejoicing that the great father has sent down rain.'

'The record jacket says it's a war chant.'

'You may believe what you wish, Bwana.'

'You're a fraud, Tuppence.'

The record went on, and Tuppence went on dancing, and I moved around the room turning off lights until only the shallow glow of one small lamp illuminated the room. My couch is one of those clever contrivances that turns into a bed when the occasion demands it. The occasion demanded it, so I pulled the proper levers and effected the desired metamorphosis. Then Miss T'pani Ngawa changed the leitmotif of the dance slightly, incorporating within the structure of basic African tribal rhythms certain dance patterns generally associated in times past with Union City, New Jersey.

Which is to say that she took off all her clothes.

'Bwana approve?'

'Bwana approve.'

'Ah! What Bwana doing?'

'Bwana going to integrate you,' I said.

'Oh, wow—'

Her skin was black velvet. I stroked her and she purred. 'We are about to miscegenate,' I explained.

'Oh, groovy,' she said 'Oh, like, wow. Bwana sure do know how to miscegenate. Oooo—'

*   *   *

Minna was particularly regal the next morning. She comes by it honestly, being the sole living descendant of Mindaugas, the last (and only) king of independent Lithuania. Mindaugas shuffled off this mortal coil some seven centuries ago, and with Lithuania incorporated in the Union of Soviet Socialist Republics, there's no overwhelming demand for Lithuanian queens. When I first found her in Lithuania, Minna was being kept in a cheerless basement room by a pair of old maids who calmly awaited the restoration of the monarchy. I smuggled her home with me, and since then she's been queening it in my apartment. She refuses to go to school, turns aside all thoughts of placing her in a foster home, chatters now and then in Lithuanian or New York English or Puerto Rican Spanish, and is generally fun to have around.

'I'm glad you're going to live with us,' she told Tuppence gravely. 'Evan says that a child needs both a mother and a father. Can you cook?'

'Not very well.'

'I suppose you can learn, though. Where are you from?'

'Kenya.'

'That's in Africa,' Minna said. 'I learned that from Evan's books. He has thousands of books and he said I can read as many as I want. I learn a lot of things from them. More than I would learn in school. Mikey says that school is a crock of shit, but I'm not supposed to say that. Mikey lives downstairs. I don't have to go to school.'

'You'll start school in the fall,' I said

She ignored me. 'This is a good place to live,' she told Tuppence. 'I'm sure you'll like it here. Can't you cook anything?'

'Just human flesh.'

'Human flesh?'

'That's all we eat in Africa. Human flesh.'

'I think,' Minna said carefully, 'that you're putting me on.'

Tuppence laughed.

'Central Park is only a few blocks from here,' Minna went on. 'There's a zoo there, but you can't go by yourself. It's not allowed. It's a children's zoo, you see, and adults are not allowed.'

'Oh.'

'They can only go,' she said, 'if they are accompanied by a child. If you'd like, Tuppence, I could accompany you. I mean, I've been to the zoo before, of course, but since you can't go without a child, I would be willing to accompany you.'

'Why, that's very sweet of you, Minna.'

'Just let me comb my hair.' Minna's hair is

long and blonde and very fine, and has a tendency to snarl. 'I wish my hair were like yours. I bet you never have to comb it, do you?'

'Never.'

'You're lucky,' Minna said. 'You're nice. I'm glad you're going to live with us.' She smiled at me. 'I'll be back soon, Evan. I have to take Tuppence to the zoo.'

*   *   *

Tuppence did not live with us, of course. She had an apartment of her own and a job of her own and a life of her own, and we both felt it would be best to keep it that way. Her quartet got a three-week engagement at a downtown club, and sometimes I would pick her up after work and bring her back to 107th Street, and sometimes she would drop up during the day, generally getting trapped into taking Minna to the zoo. I was pretty busy myself around that time. I worked up a doctoral thesis (price—$1000) for a lazy graduate student at NYU on the socioeconomic implications of the Boxer Rebellion and wrote articles (no payment) for the Journal of Armenian Studies, the United Irishman, and several East European exile newsletters. I went to a great many meetings, listened to learn-a-language records, and read and replied to the great volume of mail, which makes me my mailman's least favorite client. I

24

sent money to Greece, to be smuggled into Yugoslavian Macedonia for my son, Todor. I received a coded newsletter from a friend in Bulgaria, decoded it, and had it mimeographed for dissemination to Bulgar exiles in the States. I did, in short, the things I usually do, and a month went by as months usually go by, and then Tuppence dropped in one afternoon and told me she was leaving the country.

'A State Department tour,' she said. 'Deluxe treatment all the way. Manila, Tokyo, Hong Kong, and Bangkok. This chick is going a long way from Nairobi, baby.'

'It sounds good. When do you leave?'

'Four days from tomorrow. Got to get a few dozen shots. Plague and cholera and all those good things. They threaten to make like a pincushion out of me, man. Then we get on a jet and fly. Big bird go over great water. Bangkok—do you believe it? It sounds dirty.'

'You have an obscene mind.'

'I'm hip, and don't you love it? We're supposed to have a command performance for the King of Thailand. The word is that he's a swinger. He plays the clarinet or some such. Can you feature the king himself sitting in and wailing, and this little girl vocalizing? A long long way from Nairobi. Wow!'

She sat down, then hopped up again and did a fast two-step. 'This State Department cat mentioned something about going to Vietnam to entertain the troops, and Jimmy wanted to know which side. He said he'd rather entertain the Vietcong. Then the little State Department cat got very much up tight about things, like his face was bleached, and Kendall told him Jimmy was just joking, that it was his sense of humor. Mr. State Department gave the kind of laugh that means he didn't think it was funny, but everything stayed cool. After he split, Kendall was about ready to kill Jimmy for almost queering the whole arrangement. Jimmy said he didn't like to compromise his political beliefs, and Kendall said that for a tour of the Far East he'd paint himself red, white, and blue if they wanted. Do you think it's true what they say about Oriental men?'

'I thought it was Oriental girls that they say it about and I don't think it's true anyway.'

'Well, I suspect I'll find out.'

'Oh, I'm sure you will.'

She sat down again. 'Now you know I'll always be true to you, Bwana Evan.'

'Oh, will you?'

'Mmmm.'

*   *   *

I saw her plane off at Kennedy Airport. There was a postcard from Manila, another from Tokyo, and a third from Hong Kong. I finished up the doctoral thesis, went to more meetings, and did a lot of reading. Then I got an odd

26

letter from Bangkok:

Bwana Evan:
   Bangkok is a gas but the bread is running low. It looks as though I'll maybe have to sell my jewelry. As you know I have a very valuable collection. Do you have contacts that will prove helpful? Please let me know.
                                                    2d

My first reaction—that Tuppence had lost her mind somewhere between New York and Bangkok—gave way to a feeling of general bewilderment. When one lives in a world of secret societies and underground political movements, and does odd jobs for a nameless U.S. undercover agency, one becomes accustomed to finding meanings in apparently meaningless messages. I read her letter over and over and decided that, if there was any hidden kernel of sense to it, I couldn't spot it for the time being. Tuppence had a pair of long gold hoop earrings, and as far as I knew, that was the extent of her jewelry. Obviously jewelry was a euphemism for something, but I didn't know what, and in the meantime there was nothing to do about it. We had joked about getting her a ruby to wear in her navel. Maybe that was what she was referring to. I didn't know, and I stopped thinking about it.
   Until two days later *The Times* ran a story on page five that stated that the Royal Gem

Collection of Thailand had been stolen in its entirety, that the thief or thieves had made good their escape, that it may or may not have been an inside job, and that preliminary estimates placed the value of the gems in excess of a quarter of a million dollars.

And a day after that, while I was still recovering from that one, Tuppence and the quartet made the front page of *The Times*. *Thai Communists Kidnap American Jazz Quartet, Kenyan Singer*, said the headline, and the body copy went on to elaborate. The Kendall Bayard Quartet and Miss T'pani Ngawa, in Bangkok for a command performance before His Majesty the King of Thailand, had been snatched from their accommodations at the Hotel Orient. The kidnapping appeared to be the work of Communist guerrillas based in Northern Thailand, and it was suspected that the five kidnap victims had been spirited away to the north.

The Times made no connection between the disappearance of Tuppence and the quartet and the theft of the royal gem collection.

But I did.

CHAPTER THREE

'This is for plague,' the doctor said. 'Wouldn't care to get that, would you, now? Little red blotches, black boils under your arms, altogether most unpleasant. Never had a case of plague myself. Think everyone ought to get inoculated against it, whether traveling or not. Suppose the enemy used germ warfare, eh? Wouldn't be enough serum to go around. But an ounce of prevention . . .'

He stuck an ounce of prevention into my left arm. It hurt but seemed a healthy alternative to bubonic plague. He extracted the needle and dabbed at me with a cotton swab.

'Now the other arm. That's right, good. Rather give you the shots a week apart so as to leave you with one workable arm, but time is of the essence, isn't that what they say? This one's for cholera, and it's rather a massive inoculation, isn't it? Now, all that serum has to go into your arm. Size of the needle worries a good many people. It doesn't bother you, now, does it?'

'Uh,' I said.

'Nasty business, cholera. Dreary thing. With a decent public health program, every man, woman, and child in America would be inoculated against it. Imagine what a little flask of cholera bacilli in a reservoir would do. Eh? Thousands of people burning up with fever, dying like flies in the city streets. Makes you think, doesn't it?'

He emptied the syringe into my right arm. It was worse than the plague shot. After he removed the needle and swabbed the puncture, I concentrated very hard and managed to wiggle my fingers. I felt very proud of myself.

'Let's see, now,' he said. 'How long since your last rabies shot?'

'Pardon?'

'Rabies. Hydrophobia. Hellish proposition, that. Get yourself bitten by a dog, and you have to take the Pasteur series. Dreadfully painful. Some fourteen injections into the stomach, and if you happen to be allergic to the Pasteur shots, why, they kill you. And if you wait for symptoms of rabies to develop, by the time they appear, then death is inevitable. And one simple injection every two or three years provides complete immunity.'

'Somehow I don't think—'

'One shot does the trick. Of course no one expects to get bitten by a dog. Doesn't have to be a dog. Squirrels, foxes, raccoons—anything. Rabies is endemic in skunks, for example. Bet you never knew that.'

I hadn't.

'Don't even have to get bitten. Take a walk through a bat-infested cave and you can pick

30

up the disease from bat droppings. Just breathe it in, never even know you're exposed until it's too late. Grisly.'

'I don't have an arm left.'

'Don't give the shot in the arm. Base of the brain, same as with a dog. Good protection.'

'I don't think—'

'Every dog gets it, and they don't complain. Only take a minute.'

I managed to get out of there without his sticking a needle into my head. Both arms ached, and his conversation had very nearly turned my stomach. I walked quickly home. I passed half a dozen dogs en route, ranging in size from a miniature poodle who yipped nervously to a Doberman who maintained a watchful silence. I gave them all a wide berth and didn't get bitten once.

*   *   *

Basic arrangements were simple enough. My greatest problem was Minna, who of course wanted to come along. Tuppence was her friend, she insisted. She liked Tuppence and wanted to help her. Besides, I might get into trouble without her assistance. I would never be able to visit the Bangkok children's zoo.

Once she realized that nothing would persuade me to take her, she decided she could manage in the apartment by herself. She had friends in the building, she assured me, and her presence would facilitate such matters as the proper reception of mail and phone messages. I packed a suitcase for her and bundled her onto the subway, and we rode to Brooklyn, where a girl named Kitty Bazerian lives with her mother and grandmother. Kitty bellydances in Chelsea nightclubs as Alexandra the Great, and had already met and liked Minna. She was generally at home during the daytime, she told me, and her mother, a waitress, was home nights, and her grandmother, confined to a wheelchair, was home all the time.

Minna endured the subway ride stoically, walked through the streets of Brooklyn with the contempt of a native-born Manhattanite, and then became quite enchanted with the notion of spending a few weeks with Kitty and her family. The grandmother would teach her Armenian, she announced, and the mother would teach her to make Armenian coffee, and Kitty would teach her to dance.

'You're kind of skinny for it,' Kitty said. 'But we'll see.'

I went to the Thai consulate to have my passport stamped with a visa. I went to Air India and booked a flight to Bangkok with interim stops at San Francisco, Honolulu, and Tokyo. At Deak and Company on Times Square I turned some American money into Siamese bahts. The baht was holding firm at 4.78 U.S. cents, the clerk told me. On West

45th Street I visited a rare coin dealer and bought a couple hundred dollars' worth of common gold coins, mostly British sovereigns. The baht is a relatively stable currency, and the American dollar is highly desirable, but gold is good anywhere, at any time. And Bangkok is a center for the illicit trade in precious metals. Gold or silver may be exchanged there for anything—teen-age concubines, opium, guns, anything.

At my apartment I tucked the cash into a flat nylon money belt and fastened it around my waist beneath my clothing. The gold pieces, twenty-two of them, fit into the casing of a flashlight battery with just a little room left. I added cotton to fill and put the battery back in the flashlight. I was packing the flashlight and a variety of other things in a pair of suitcases when the phone rang.

I answered it, and a girl with a French or Belgian accent wanted to know if I was the Blue Star Hand Laundry. I said I wasn't, and the girl said she simply had to get in touch with the Blue Star Hand Laundry, and hung up.

At the beginning, when the Chief first started using me for unusual assignments, I often failed to get the point of odd calls like that. My natural impulse, when some clown gets a wrong number, is to hang up, sometimes with a friendly word, sometimes with a curse. The Chief—I don't know his name or exactly what he does, but he seems to think I work for

33

him, and now and then I do—the Chief, at any rate, is indefatigable. He knows that the CIA taps my phone and the FBI reads my mail (or else it's the other way around), so he sends me cryptic messages that may or may not fool the CIA and the FBI but that almost always fool me. Once an operative of his had to hand me a gum wrapper twice before I finally read the little message on it instead of flipping it into a litter basket.

This time, though, I understood immediately. I picked up the Manhattan yellow pages and looked up laundries and found a listing for the Blue Star Hand Laundry at 666 Fifth Avenue. Since it seemed unlikely that some mad Chinaman would open a laundry, hand or otherwise, in the Tishman Building, I guessed that the Blue Star was a telephone front for the Chief's organization, whatever it might be.

So I closed the yellow pages and went on packing. There was no point in answering him. He would probably want to send me sneaking off to Poland or Hungary on some unpleasant task, and I couldn't because I had to go to Siam. I didn't want to try telling him why I had to go to Siam. I didn't want to tell him anything at all. I wanted to wait for the fifty-six hours before I could board my Air India flight and then, as unobtrusively as possible, I wanted to fly to Bangkok.

I finished packing. The phone rang again,

and it was the same woman, but this time she had an Italian accent. Sometimes the Chief has all the subtlety of a pneumatic hammer. I said, 'No, damn it, you have the wrong number,' and added a string of curses in Italian, which I rather hoped she understood. I banged the phone down and when it rang again twenty minutes later, I let it ring. I stayed in the apartment for four hours, and the silly phone went on ringing intermittently. I found that it took a startling amount of willpower to ignore a ringing telephone. This should not be so; the simple fact that some dolt possesses one's phone number and a dime should not compel one to answer the thing. But we are all of us brothers of Pavlov's dogs, quick to respond to that bell, with feet and hands if not with saliva; held captive, too, by the idiot notion that the call might be Something Important. After four hours I couldn't stand it any more. I left the apartment and went out for a walk.

Some nut followed me.

I may have been followed before, but this was the first time I ever realized it. When I left the building, there was a short, dumpy, middle-aged fellow on the other side of the street. He was watching some of the neighborhood kids play stickball. I walked uptown on Broadway and stopped for coffee at a Nedick's and I saw him again, studying ties in a store window. I didn't really pay much attention to him. I doubled back to the apartment to pick up a book I'd been reading on nationalism in the Far East, and when I came out, there he was back at his first post, watching the stickball game. When I saw him for the third time, I decided that it was an odd coincidence and I kept an eye out for him from then on. He wasn't very good; after that, every time I turned around, there he was.

I wondered to whom he belonged. If he was from the CIA or something like that, I could let him follow me forever, and it wouldn't much matter. If he was one of the Chief's men, and this seemed more likely, then sooner or later he would make contact. That was the last thing I wanted. I could always lose him, I thought, but I would have to do so in innocent and casual fashion or the Chief would wonder why I was ducking him.

I used the subway, slipping through the door at 59th Street at the last moment, as if I had almost forgotten my stop. It was a nice try, but my man had been standing near another door and just made it out in time. I went upstairs and jumped in a cab, and he caught another cab and stayed right behind me. That there should be two empty cabs on hand at that hour struck me as a piece of particularly bad luck. I let my cabby take me down to the Village. The other cab followed close behind.

In a coffeehouse on Macdougal Street, nearly empty in the late afternoon, I scribbled furiously on a paper napkin. He came in right on my heels, caught my eye, winked. He had to be one of the Chief's men, I decided, and he was ready to make contact.

He took a table near mine. I stood up, walked past his table, dropped the napkin in front of him, and kept going to the lavatory. The writing on the napkin said, *There's someone following both of us. I'm going to skip—cover me.*

I glanced back at him. He winked at me again, crumpled the paper napkin, and turned a wary eye on the doorway. He would stay there like a faithful guard dog until I dropped his leash.

Now, I thought, it would be simple. I had invented a fairly plausible reason for my own departure; I wasn't ducking out on him but on someone else. I locked myself in the john. The window opened out on an alleyway that cut across to Minetta Lane. All I had to do was climb through it.

I spent five minutes struggling with that window. I don't think it had ever been opened since they built the building. They certainly hadn't done so when they painted the last time, or since then, because the damned thing had been painted shut. When someone began knocking impatiently on the john door, I gave up and went back to my table. My shadow was where I had left him. He said in a whisper, 'The Chief—'

'No time,' I said. 'C'mon, cover me.'

37

I left, and he walked beside me. We headed south toward Bleecker. He looked around, then spoke to me out of the corner of his mouth. He said, 'Who's on our tail?'

There were two boys in field jackets a few paces behind us. Near them was a long-haired girl carrying a guitar. Behind her a young executive type with attaché case.

'The one with the briefcase,' I said.

'I didn't notice him before.'

'Surprising. He was on me while you were watching the kids playing stickball.'

'Never even spotted him,' he whispered. 'You go ahead, Tanner. I'll take him out.'

I kept walking. My erstwhile tail slipped into the shadows of a doorway, let the two beat types and the guitarist pass him, then moved out just in time to get a foot in front of the young executive, who promptly dropped the attaché case and sprawled on top of it.

'Clumsy bastard,' said my tail. The executive apologized, and my man roared, 'Watch what you say about my mother, fella!' and hit him in the side of the jaw, and I ducked around the corner on Bleecker and caught another taxi.

*   *   *

I spent the rest of my waiting time with Ramon and Felicidad Abrillo. Ramon is an old-line syndicalist who left Spain after the Civil War and who occasionally boarded Spanish anarchists and Trotskyists who were in the States illegally. He let me spend the next two days in his apartment and he sent his nephew Felipe to fetch my bags from my place. I ate paella with eels, read books in Spanish and English, listened to recorded flamenco music, and remained pleasantly incommunicado.

*　　　*　　　*

My flight was scheduled to leave Kennedy Airport at 11:35 Thursday night. I took a taxi to the airport and checked my bags at the Air India flight desk. On my way to the passengers' lounge a fat man with a wide striped tie collided with me. I said, 'Sorry,' and he said, 'Go to the men's room, Tanner.'

I looked at my watch. My flight would be boarding in twenty minutes. I could brazen it out, go to the lounge and try to get to my plane before they bothered me any more. Or would the Chief have the plane stopped? It was possible. Anything was possible.

But I really didn't want to talk to him. I headed on toward the flight lounge and as I approached the desk I reached into my breast pocket for my ticket, and it wasn't there.

Beautiful.

So I went to the men's room. The Chief was there, washing his pudgy hands at the sink. As usual he was wearing an expensively tailored suit that did not fit well on his plump frame.

He smiled broadly at me, then began drying his hands with one of those machines that blows hot, moist air at one.

'We're quite alone,' he said. 'We may talk.'

'Anyone could walk in—'

'Not at all. One of the lads will hang an out-of-order sign on the door. There's your ticket, by the way.'

He nodded at it, and I went over and collected it from the shelf over the sink.

He said, 'You led us a chase, Tanner. Bangkok, eh? What's in Bangkok?'

'It's just a personal trip.'

He chuckled. 'Oh, come, now, Tanner,' he said. 'I know you better than that. Why didn't you make contact?'

'I was being followed. I didn't want to risk it.'

'You could have given us a call, you know.' He was still drying his hands. Those machines never work particularly well and occasionally don't work at all, but the places that provide them often don't have towels, so one has no choice. He kept rubbing his hands together in the air spray. Finally he gave up and wiped them on his pants.

'All I wanted to know,' he said peevishly, 'is why you're going to Bangkok. It's not as though I had some other place to send you. Things are rather quiet at the moment, as a matter of fact. But when one of my boys heads for Southeast Asia, I do like to know about it.'

'Well—'

'I like to encourage individual initiative, Tanner. You know that. My men don't type up reports, they don't have to clear it with me before they clean their fingernails. Nothing of the sort. I never tell a man how to do something. I rarely ask how it was done.'

'I know.'

'But Bangkok is a forbidding place, you know. And, while my men are on their own, sometimes it's possible for one to give another a hand. Why are you going to Thailand?'

'I have a few contacts there.'

'I'm not surprised. You appear to have contacts everywhere. Go on.'

'You know, of course, that Bangkok is a center of the narcotics trade. Raw opium from Red China is processed there into morphine and heroin. I understand that something like forty percent of the illicit heroin supply passes through Thailand.'

'I didn't realize it was that much.'

Neither did I, but it seemed like a good working figure. 'Some people I know, friends, actually, have been exploring the possibilities of launching a large-scale opium operation in one of the new African states.'

'Refining it?'

'The whole operation. Growing it *and* processing it.' I glanced at him, and he seemed very interested. I was encouraged. 'They need connections with purchasers, of course, and

41

they need details on processing and distribution, all of that. Of course the opium trade is very important economically to Peking. If the Chinese growers suddenly found themselves operating in a competitive market—'

'Interesting,' he said.

'I don't suppose much will really come of it.' Nothing, I thought, could possibly come of it. 'But it seemed worth the trip. As I said, I know a few people in Bangkok. I can get a certain amount of access to some peripheral figures in the opium market. But I don't want anyone to know the purpose of the trip.'

'Of course not. You'll have a good many hostile forces to contend with, won't you? The Chinese, the Thai refiners, just about everyone connected with the Bangkok operation.' He thought for a moment. 'Well, you'll need a cover. Bangkok swarms with agents these days. Half the town spies for the CIA and the other half spies *on* it. Let me see now. The Agency will have to know about you—'

'But—'

'No, no, they'll be onto you at once anyway. Best if they have advance information. We'll leak it to them that you're connected with a pilot study of guerrilla activity in Thailand. How does that sound? We're thinking of increasing the U.S. military commitment to Thailand, and you're being sent there to determine how acute the situation is. They've been doing the same thing, of course, and they'll think you're being sent to determine the accuracy of their reports. They'll never guess your major interest is opium.' He lit a cigarette. 'Of course this is just the sort of operation the Agency would like to take over for its very own, and you could imagine what they would do with it. If it ever got out that agents of the U.S. Government were helping to establish a narcotics industry in Africa, it would be hell, and the Agency can't seem to do anything without splashing it all across the world press. I can see why you've emphasized secrecy. Which new African state, by the way?'

'I'm not certain.'

'You don't even want to tell me, eh?' He chuckled. 'Probably not a bad idea. You'd better go now, they'll be calling your flight any moment. Incidentally, you got our man in a bit of a jam. That fellow he tackled wasn't following you at all.'

'Oh? I could have sworn—'

'And his attaché case spilled open in the ruckus, and it turned out that it was filled with obscene photographs. The police arrested the fellow, and our lad has to be a witness at the trial. He'd been planning a little trip south of the border, and now this. Just an inconvenience, but it shows the way things can go awry for the oddest reasons.' He checked his watch. 'Better get on that plane,' he said. 'I'll just duck in here for a moment.' And he locked himself into one of the toilet stalls so that no one would see him when I opened the door.

I boarded my plane with a few minutes to spare. A doe-eyed stewardess with a half-moon on her forehead bowed me to my seat. The takeoff was reassuringly uneventful. I leaned back in my seat and thought about the cover story I had invented for the Chief and the cover story he in turn had devised for the CIA. Opium and guerrillas. Mine seemed even less plausible than his, but it was close.

But consider reality—I was rushing in, a little higher than the fools, a little lower than the angels, to liberate Siamese jewels and a Kenyan jazz singer. I wasn't at all certain that the jewels and the jazz singer were together or where either of them might be found. Nor did I know just what I would do with the jewels when I found them. I had a fair idea what I'd do with Tuppence.

The passengers on either side of me fell asleep. I didn't, and envied them. The plane flew with monotonous efficiency. I thought of all the things that might go wrong, and the more I thought, the more things occurred to me. Before very long I had managed to convince myself that I'd been an absolute fool to pass up the rabies shot. There would be endless bat-infested caves in Thailand, I was certain. And dogs and raccoons and squirrels and skunks. I would get bitten by a rabid skunk. Alone in Thailand, stranded, no jewels, no Tuppence, no Pasteur shots, and cornered by a rabid skunk—

CHAPTER FOUR

I was alone in Thailand, stranded, no jewels, no Tuppence, and cornered by a rabid skunk from the Central Intelligence Agency of the United States of America.

His name was Barclay Houghton Hewlitt, and his mother must have given him three last names with clairvoyant assurance that no one would ever want to call him by a first name. He told me to call him Barclay. I didn't want to call him anything and I wished someone would call him off.

He met my plane in Bangkok, the idiot. We landed in midmorning, Thai time. I had been too long in the air and had seen the insides of too many airports to know what time it might be in New York or just how much of my life I had devoted to the process of getting from hither to yon. Somewhere along the way we had crossed the International Date Line, a concept I understand hazily in the abstract and not at all in the concrete, so it was possible, I suppose, that I had arrived in Bangkok before I left New York, and that if I continued around the world fast enough, I could get back to New

York in time to meet the Chief again in the washroom. I didn't really want to think about this and I didn't have to, because Barclay Houghton Hewlitt picked me up as I came down the ramp. He spoke my last name, and smiled, and spoke all three of his own names, followed by his organization's three initials, and told me to call him by his first name, and thrust out his hand, which I shook. A reflex, like answering telephones.

'You'll want to stay at the Orient, of course. I've booked a room for you, took the liberty. Private bath, tub *and* shower, fully air-conditioned, quite nicely furnished. Tenth floor, so you'll have a splendid view. Give you some perspective on the situation here, ha ha.'

He was small and pink. He would have looked quite pink anywhere and in Bangkok he glowed like a sore thumb. He told me that one of the boys would see to my bags, ha ha, and I said that I would just as soon see to my own bags, ha ha.

'Oh, ho, ho, I guess you would. Top secret and all that, eh? You haff zee documents, ha ha?'

They unloaded the airplane, and I collected my baggage and followed it through Customs. A narrow, bespectacled Thai asked me to open my bags, and Barclay Houghton Hewlitt began waving cards at him, dropping winks at him, and urging him to let me through directly.

The Customs man said he would have to

clear this with a superior. People were beginning to pay far too much attention to us. Already, as a result of Barclay Houghton Hewlitt's greeting, at least half the population of Bangkok knew who I was and what I was supposed to be doing there. Now the fool would only succeed in assuring them that I had something classified in my baggage, with the result that my room would be searched and something, no doubt, stolen.

I opened the suitcases. The Thai, perhaps to save face, went through everything. There was not much beyond clothing and toilet articles. He picked up the flashlight and hefted it.

'Damned silly,' Hewlitt said. 'We could have avoided all this, Tanner. Hardly a royal welcome for you, ha ha.'

The Thai unscrewed the back of the flashlight and poured the batteries into his hand. One dropped and bounced on the floor. I closed my eyes briefly. When I opened them, the Thai had recovered the battery from the floor and was replacing it and its fellow in the flashlight. He replaced the cap and flicked the switch. Predictably, nothing happened.

'Must have put the damned things in backwards,' Hewlitt said. 'You fouled up the man's flashlight, son. If you're bent on wasting everyone's time, why not waste some of your own and repair the damage? I'm sure it functioned properly before you—'

Barclay Houghton Hewlitt. We got the

suitcases repacked and left the Customs shed without further incident. The taxi Hewlitt had waiting was no longer waiting. We got another one, eventually, and proceeded directly to the Hotel Orient. The streets in the central part of the city were crowded, more with bicycles and pedestrians than with cars, and our taxi moved slowly and tentatively through the maze.

I had never been to the Far East before. I could speak and understand the language, but I had never before heard it as a city's background music, humming around me as verbal white noise. Every city has its own music and its own smells, and I would have to get the feel of this one if I was to accomplish anything in it. I rolled down my window and looked and listened, and BHH of CIA did what he could to spoil it by supplying a running commentary 'Just to help you get your bearings locally—ha ha.'

The Hotel Orient was steel and glass on the outside, nylon and plastic within. The entire staff and most of the guests spoke English. My room had a thick carpet, a huge bed, and an air-conditioning unit that had rendered it uncomfortably cold. I turned it off and opened the window, and Hewlitt looked at me as though I had left my mind somewhere over the Pacific Ocean.

While I unpacked my suitcases and put things away Hewlitt babbled. He was personally so pleased I had come. The situation in Thailand was crucial, no doubt about it. A good government, a good solid government, but one had to keep on one's toes, ha ha. Of course the Agency kept close tabs on everything. The Agency liked to maintain a position of dominance in Thailand. This was Marlboro country, ha ha. Good, though, that I was coming around to dig up data and present an impartial report. And of course they would be glad to ease the way for me, make sure I saw the right people and had easy access to the right data. The correct data, that was to say, ha ha. There would be a car and a driver at my disposal, needless to say, and if I wanted appointments with any officials in the Thai government, why, I need only ask, and in fact they had taken the liberty of arranging a luncheon with . . .

I suddenly saw how I had been cast. I was the Junketing Congressman, out to have a Good Time and get the Big Picture, and to be Handled with Kid Gloves, and Supervised to Death. The cover that had been provided for me was grand protection; it fit me like a noose. I had been ostensibly dispatched to study a CIA operation and return with conclusions that would either confirm or conflict with their own, and the chances of their leaving me alone were about as good as the chance of Barclay Houghton Hewlitt ending a sentence without a nervous little laugh.

I had to get the clown off my back.

'I've spent too much time on planes,' I told him, cutting in between one ha and another, 'I need a shower and a shave and a good ten hours of sleep. Leave a number where I can reach you.'

I had evidently hit the right tone. He scampered. That was just what he did. He left his card and he started to say something but stopped, and then he scampered.

*   *   *

I had the shower and the shave, but instead of the ten hours of sleep I'd mentioned to Hewlitt, I stretched out on the bed and watched the ceiling for twenty minutes. I needed a place to start, and Abel Vaudois seemed promising. He was a Swiss who divided his time between Bangkok and Macao, buying and selling almost anything. We had corresponded a few years earlier when I had written him on behalf of the Latvian Army-in-Exile to inquire into the possibility of running guns into the Baltic States. Vaudois had been very cooperative, and seemed delighted to know of the existence of the Latvian Army-in-Exile, an organization hitherto unknown to him. Since then we had exchanged perhaps half a dozen letters, and although I had serious doubts that we would ever launch a revolution in Latvia, I felt I could call on him for information. If anything valuable was stolen

50

anywhere in the Orient, there was a fair chance that he would know something about it.

I put on clean clothes and rode the elevator downstairs to the lobby. Hewlitt was sitting on a lounge chair with the Far East edition of *Time* on his lap. I got back into the elevator and went back to my room.

This, I thought, would never do. I called room service and asked for a bellhop, and a slim-hipped boy appeared shortly thereafter at my door. 'A special favor,' I said, and passed him some Siamese notes. He made them disappear. His smile was eloquent.

'Gill?' he said hopefully. 'Yun gill?'

'Just a favor.' In Siamese I explained that there was a gentleman in the lobby whom I rather wished to avoid. Was there, perhaps, a service entrance through which I might leave the hotel?

There was, he told me. He would have to go to another room to pick up a breakfast tray but if he might return in a moment, he would be pleased to lead me to the service entrance.

He was back a few moments later. I followed him down the corridor to the freight elevator and rode downstairs along with a stack of folding chairs. The elevator wheezed and creaked. We went straight on down to the basement and made our way through a maze of packing cases and garbage cans into the underground parking area. At the foot of the ramp I handed my guide a few more bahts. His smile widened. I left him and climbed the ramp and stepped out into the sunlight.

I turned left, walked half a block, and heard a familiar voice at my elbow. 'I say there, Tanner. Couldn't sleep after all, eh? Luck running into you like this, ha ha. Ready for lunch? Fine little place just around the corner, nothing fancy, ha ha, but they serve a fine businessman's lunch.'

My lunch consisted of a glass of unidentifiable fruit juice, a plate of excellent spiced beef and rice, a root vegetable that tasted a little like parsnips, and a dreary dish of caramel custard. My tea was jasmine-scented and very strong. I would have enjoyed the meal a good deal more if I had been alone. But Barclay Houghton Hewlitt, ha ha, was a constant reminder of the bellhop's perfidy. He was a perfect gentleman, never mentioning the fact that I had tried to dodge him. And he picked up the tab, which seemed no more than fair—I had spent more than the cost of the lunch on the treacherous bellhop.

I wondered if the boy had been merely enterprising or whether he was a regular employee of the CIA. After lunch, wandering through the narrow streets of Bangkok with Hewlitt, I began to get the feeling that half the town consisted of more or less regular employees of the Agency. Hewlitt went on pointing out drops and meeting places and fronts—a travel agency, a tobbo shop, a cocktail lounge, a restaurant—all, he assured me, fully staffed by competent Agency personnel. I'm not certain whether he was trying to reassure me of his outfit's competence in Thailand or to warn me of the impossibility of slipping my leash. Perhaps a little of both, ha ha.

What really bothered me, though, was the great quantity of people who were watching us. An unusual number of natives and Westerners were taking a surreptitious interest in Barclay Houghton Hewlitt and me. We were followed, studied, glanced at, appraised, and, I'm sure, photographed time and time again. It seemed highly unlikely that all of the watchbirds could be CIA people. There would be agents of other powers as well—French and British and Russian and what BHH called Chicoms. And, given the sort of city Bangkok had become, there would be no end of freelance operatives and double agents and triple agents ad infinitum.

In the middle of the afternoon I developed a convenient headache and had to return to the hotel. Hewlitt, who would have made a dandy shepherd, escorted me to the Orient in a taxi. I called down for a bottle of Scotch and some ice. The same bellhop brought my order, and he and I both pretended we had never met before. I tipped him not at all.

If he had been my size, I would have taken the Scotch bottle and clouted him over the

53

head. I wouldn't have done this purely out of animosity, nor was it some gentlemanly restraint on my part that let his size protect him. But I could have used bellhop's livery in my size. If they were going to keep a batch of men on me, some sort of disguise would help. A uniform provides the best sort of anonymity, but I would have had to lose many pounds and shrink many inches to fit into his.

I sat around the room drinking until it was time for dinner. The hotel restaurant had a French chef who did a creditable job with coq au vin. I thought of going backstage to compliment him in person, buying his white coat and hat, and slipping out through the staff entrance. Instead I went back to my room and put in a little more time with the whiskey bottle.

Around nine thirty I left the hotel. Barclay Houghton Hewlitt had departed, but there were at least two men on me, perhaps more. I wandered aimlessly around the downtown district, and a stiff-spined American and a slouching Thai both kept me under rather close observation. I was not sure whose side they were on. The question seemed academic. The night air was warm and damp, the sky clear. The keyed-up atmosphere of daytime Bangkok had yielded place to a gently throbbing aura of sweet decadence. The air did not actually smell of incense, but one felt that it ought to. Innocent doorways managed to convey the impression that opium dens lay within. I walked farther south and passed bars filled with U.S. military personnel. American jazz blared forth from American jukeboxes.

I went into a darkened nightclub on the Street of the Seven Sisters. The hostess who took me to my seat had her skirt slit almost to her waist. A waitress in sequined panties and halter brought a drink that was mostly water. The music was recorded, the stripper uninspired. I might as well have gone to Chicago.

A girl came to my table. She was dark and slender, her eyes many years older than the rest of her face. She said, 'You buy me drink, soldier?'

I nodded. The waitress appeared almost immediately, put the usual B-girl drink in front of my new friend, and took some of my money. My girl gulped her drink and put her hand on my leg.

'I like you,' she said.

I found that difficult to believe.

'You like me?'

'Sure.'

'You want go upstairs? Very special place.'

'Well—'

'Do fuck-fuck with me.'

I looked around. My Siamese tail was at the bar, my American a few tables away. Both were being very careful not to look directly at me. I turned my eyes to the girl, who was

55

giving some details of just how glorious it would be to accept her suggestion. She was a pretty thing, quite full in the breasts for such a slender girl, with skin of a warm golden brown. I wondered if there was a polite way to tell a girl that one did not want to do fuck-fuck with her. *I am sorry, my dear, but I was, uh, wounded in the war*— No, that wasn't quite right.

'We go upstairs now?'

'Fine,' I said.

I followed her between the tiny tables, around the side of the stage. We climbed a flight of stairs and walked down a corridor between a row of closed doors, from behind most of which the sounds of giggling and/or passion could be heard. She opened a door and led me into a very small room, almost all of which was taken up by a rather large bed. The bed had seen considerable use since last its sheets had been changed.

She closed the door. 'Six dollar American,' she said.

I walked around the bed. The room was at the back of the building, and the window opened on a narrow airshaft. My tails would be waiting for me downstairs. They would stay where they were until the girl reappeared. Of course there was always the chance that she was an agent for someone or other. But if I could get out the window—

'Six dollar, honey. Then fuck-fuck.'

I turned to her. She had taken off all her

clothes, which is to say that she had removed her dress. She had a lovely little body. I took a ten-dollar bill from my wallet.

'You no have six dollar? I have to get change later—'

'Are you Siamese?'

'I am Siamese, honey, but I am no twin.' She said this with a hopeful smile that indicated she had no idea what it meant, but some soldier had taught her it was funny.

In her own language I said, 'There are men downstairs who would do evil to me. I must leave by this window. You may keep the entire ten dollars. Remain in this room for some time after I have gone.'

She looked at me, then down at herself. 'You speak Siamese,' she said.

'Yes.'

'You do not wish to make love with me? There is something wrong?'

'I have to—'

She put her hands on her breasts. 'You want another girl? I will get another girl if you wish it. You prefer a boy?'

I took her shoulders in my hands. 'You are most beautiful. Your body is pleasingly shaped, and you have a good aroma. But I am in danger and must ask your help. When I return to you, then there shall be a time for lovemaking.'

'Ah.'

'Will you help me?'

57

Her eyes were different now, softer, more youthful, the brittle gloss of commercial love gone from them. 'You speak the language of Siam well. Have you been long in Bangkok?'

'I arrived today.'

'It is rare to meet an American who speaks Siamese. You have been with many Siamese girls?'

'No. I have never been with one.'

She began unbuttoning my shirt. She had tiny hands, and the tips of her fingers were very soft. 'First be with me,' she said. 'Be with me, then I will help you.'

It was the language that made the difference. In English, with all her talk of fuck-fuck, I had found her quite lacking in allure; she had then matched the dirty bed and the sordid little room. Now, speaking naturally in the liquid tones of her own tongue, she was somehow more a woman and less a whore.

And, after all, her body was pleasingly shaped, and she had a good aroma.

I undressed. She draped my shirt over the lamp so that the room was filled with a dim light. In bed, she showed herself to be a creature of great wisdom, given to clever movements of hands and body and possessed of enviable muscular control.

Afterward we took the sheet from the bed and tied one end of it to the bed rail. I kissed her, and we told each other how much pleasure we had found together. Then I let myself out the window on the sheet. It carried me most of the way to the ground, and I dropped the rest of the way without spraining an ankle. She pulled the sheet back inside the window and blew me a kiss.

'Stay in the room for another ten minutes.'

'I shall.'

'Good-bye, my love.'

'Take care, my cherished darling.'

I threaded my way through an accumulation of defenestrated garbage to an alley alongside a building at the far end of the airshaft. I hoped she would wait at least a few minutes before going downstairs to select another cherished darling. Or would she be downstairs already, prepared to sell me out?

I darted through the alleyway and emerged on a street I hadn't been on before. A cab cruised by almost at once, and I hailed it and gave the driver Abel Vaudois' address.

No one followed us.

CHAPTER FIVE

'I will be able to learn some of what you wish to know, my little Evan. The information industry is of prime importance in Bangkok, and my sources are of the best. But if you will accept some advice in addition to what information I can supply—'

'Of course.'

'Then, it is this, and of course you are free to disregard it. But it is this—remain in Bangkok and enjoy yourself and play whatever games may amuse you with the clutch of spies who infest this city. And then, by all means, return to New York. Do not attempt to move into the north country. Bangkok is a city of great charm, of infinite sophistication. In the north are cut-throats and bandits and madmen. Whether or not many of them are Communists I do not know. They are ... what? Malcontents. And brutal fools.' He smiled disarmingly. 'You would have a far better chance, I think, of carrying out a revolution in Latvia than of completing the most innocent sort of mission in rural areas of Thailand.'

Abel Vaudois was an excellent host. We sat in the comfortable library of his immense estate and drank what was easily the best cognac I had ever tasted. His home, a rococo mansion on the eastern outskirts of Bangkok, housed Vaudois, an endless flock of servants, and his two Eurasian mistresses, each of whom presided over a separate wing of the house.

I had told him virtually everything I knew about Tuppence and the jewels. He in turn had known only a little more than I. From what he had heard so far, Tuppence and the musicians were not suspected of the theft of the gems. They had played a royal command performance at the palace, had greatly pleased His Majesty, and had returned to their hotel. The royal gem collection was stolen the following night in a daring commando-style raid in which several guards were killed, alarm systems cleverly short-circuited, and no clues left behind. Then, a day later, Tuppence and the Kendall Bayard Quartet were snatched from the Orient.

'I had suspected the gems might be offered to me,' Vaudois said. 'It would have been the sort of proposition that might have tempted me. Would I have cared to involve myself? I do not know. I live quite comfortably in Bangkok. It is a congenial atmosphere, I am at ease here. One does not wish to jeopardize such a situation. And yet'—his eyes narrowed—'and yet, the profit potential of such a theft is enormous. Few could handle the dispersal of the collection. I could do so, of course. One would have to parcel the lot, a shipment here, a shipment there, certain pieces to be broken down, certain stones to be recut . . .'

He continued, outlining the entire operation as much for his own benefit as for mine. He was a huge man, well over six feet tall and carrying a great deal of weight on a very heavy frame. Most of our conversation was conducted in French, but now and then he switched to German when he wished to make a particular point.

He rang a bell, and a servant entered

silently, poured more cognac for each of us, and departed as silently as he had come. 'You will sleep here tonight,' he said. 'I gather you have no great desire to return to your hotel?'

'None.'

'Good. I am sure you will be comfortable here, and tomorrow will be time enough to see what can be learned about your friends. And the King's gems. But tell me, have you been to Europe lately? I cannot return, as you must know. Tell me . . .'

We talked awhile of Europe, our conversation broken now and then by the bell summoning the boy with more cognac. Then we talked of the increasing complexity of international travel, of the many organizations with their extensive dossiers, of the endless paperwork involved. It had been a simpler matter in the old days of the Orient Express, he assured me. In those days the individual had been all; now everyone was a cog in a machine, a component in a computer network.

'This fool you spoke of,' he said. 'I gather he believed your tale of opium?'

'I think so.'

'Incredible. You were correct in saying that Bangkok is a center for the trade. Bangkok, Beirut, Macao, Istanbul—those four are of considerable importance. Imagine establishing an operation in Africa! I have never even heard of such an idea. One frequently hears talk of developing new refineries in the Middle

East. There was even a plan, some years ago, to attempt opium cultivation in Iraq. Some preliminary inquiries were made, and then the government changed hands and nothing ever came of it. But Africa—I wonder, now. The right climatic conditions would be found without difficulty, would you not say? Of course you would require a nation with a properly permissive government and a government with some degree of stability. A problem, that. Africa—'

'You sound interested.'

'Ah, my little Evan!' He smiled disarmingly. 'Let us say merely that I find the notion amusing.'

*   *   *

I spent the night in a comfortable bedroom on the second floor after having declined my host's offer of a parlormaid's companionship for the night. Instead I took the cognac bottle and a few books upstairs with me. I reread an early Eric Ambler novel in French. Vaudois was right, I decided—it was simpler then. I read a book on Indochina, also in French, written about the time that the French were being forced out of that unhappy land. The author had concluded that European influence could not possibly be maintained in Southeast Asia and that it ought to be yielded up as gracefully as possible. I wanted to put stamps on the book and mail it to the State Department.

The sun came up. I looked out my window at an expanse of formal gardens, lush with subtropical vegetation. The sky overhead was a brilliant blue. I waited in my room until a servant knocked to summon me to breakfast. I ate alone, and a giggling Chinese girl brought me a plate piled high with eggs and bacon and sausages and fried potatoes and a pot of particularly good coffee seasoned with chicory. I was on my third cup of coffee when Vaudois entered the room.

'I hope you found this to be a typical American breakfast?'

'A little better than that,' I said.

'Potatoes, in particular, are difficult to obtain locally. But I find them so welcome a change from the endless rice. You slept comfortably? I am glad. I have taken a liberty, Evan. I have been presumptuous. I hope you will forgive me. I sent one of my young men over to the Orient to pack your bags and bring them here. Everything awaits you in the library. It occurred to me that you might not wish to return to the hotel and the watchful eye of Mr. Hewlitt, was that his name? I would have asked you first, but this was more easily accomplished early in the morning, and I did not wish to disturb your sleep. You are not angry with me?'

'I'm delighted. I didn't want to go back to

the Orient.'

'I thought not. And now as to the jewels and your girl friend. I have made inquiries. Not productive, but not entirely fruitless either. First, the gems.' He heaved a sigh. 'The business of the theft, as you may have gathered last night, was carried out in a genuinely professional manner. And yet no local professionals in that line of work seem to have been involved. Nor have any known professional jewel thieves from outside been recognized in Bangkok of late. Nor, finally, have any of the jewels made their appearance on the international market. This last point is not of great significance, I do not think. Had I been concerned with the theft'—a wistful sigh—'I would not have attempted to disperse the gems for some time. Two or three months, at the least. Of course many persons prefer to move more rapidly. It is a question, I suspect, both of temperament and of organization.

'Now, as to the musicians—it does seem very likely that they were taken away to the north. No one to whom I spoke has heard anything about their having been taken out of the country, and my contacts might well have heard of it had it happened. You understand that in my line of business it is important to be able to enter and leave countries without going through Customs, so I have access to good information in that area. There have been no ransom attempts either.

'So I wonder immediately why anyone might kidnap them, eh? Perhaps they stole the jewels, and the kidnappers then stole them *and* the jewels. But I do not think so. Or perhaps they were kidnapped for political reasons, eh? I would not attempt to guess those reasons, but in the realm of world politics I have found it to be true that anything is possible, anything at all. As long as the motive of financial profit dominates, then a degree of logic prevails. But once political considerations are involved, ah, then lunacy and chaos enter in.' He shook his head. 'In my native Switzerland we remained quite aloof from such politics. We let our nation serve as a maze for political rats from other nations to wander through, but we ourselves were never involved.'

'But that's no longer the case,' I said.

'Oh?'

So I told him about the situation in the Jura, a few hundred square miles of the Canton of Bern bordering on France. The Jura region, predominantly French-speaking, desired to secede from the German-speaking canton and achieve autonomous status within the Swiss Confederation. Even now extremists were waging arson attacks against German-speaking inhabitants of the Jura, and political refugees were beginning to turn up in Paris.

'But this is remarkable,' Vaudois said. 'I am from the Jura. It is only since the Treaty of Vienna that we have been a part of Bern.'

'I know.'

'And they wage attacks on the German element, eh? Have they much hope for success?'

'I doubt it, but—'

'You know of these people?'

'Yes.' I hesitated. 'As a matter of fact,' I said, 'I'm a member of the Council for Autonomy of the Jura. I haven't been able to play too active a role, as it happens, but—'

'This is marvelous!' He beamed with pleasure. 'No doubt my countrymen are severely oppressed, Evan. You must supply me with a name and address. I would be honored to furnish them with, oh, a small donation.'

*   *   *

After he had recovered from his attack of Juran patriotism, I told him my plan for getting into the north. Obviously I needed a cover. Neither my size nor my complexion would facilitate my passing as a Siamese, and I would not be particularly welcome as an American agent. But throughout the remote areas of the world the natives had grown accustomed to the periodic invasions of American scientists, especially of the simpler sort. With just the most rudimentary sort of equipment I could easily pass as an itinerant lepidopterist, chasing net in hand over the rice paddies of Thailand in a madcap hunt for elusive butterflies and moths. I wouldn't even have to pursue any winged creatures. I could insist that I was only interested in the Bat-Winged Gobbletail or some such, and leave inferior species alone. And, with that sort of cover, I could visit remote villages and mingle innocently with the people, asking all sorts of irrelevant questions and trying to get a line on whatever pea-green butterflies and black people might have passed through the region.

'It is not impossible,' Abel Vaudois admitted. 'You may make a list of the various articles you require, and I will have them purchased for you. There is no sense in your showing your face in Bangkok. And of course you will want a driver. I can supply a man.'

'I can drive.'

'But your driver will also be able to speak Siamese.'

'I speak the language.'

'You do?' He studied me. 'That is hard to believe. I have lived here for years and remain at sea in it. And as you know, I am a good linguist. From birth I spoke German and French and Italian, albeit with a heavy Switzer accent. And I am fluent in several other European tongues. But this maddening language? I find it impossible. I say *khao* when I wish some rice, but the same syllable also means badly, or white, or old, or news. One little syllable with five meanings!'

'It is all a matter of inflection. For rice one

would say *khao*, for badly one would say *khao*, for news one would say *khao*, for white one would say *khao*, for old one—'

'Stop, stop! You will give me a headache. Each time it sounds quite the same to me.'

'When you have the ear for it, the words sound quite distinct.'

'And you have such an ear?'

'I can get along in Siamese.'

'Then this will be a great help to you. Ah, Evan. Should you ever tire of working for this Chief of yours—'

'I don't work for him, exactly.'

'Well, should you ever desire to work for me—'

'I am honored, Abel.'

'My good little friend. Such a madness, from Latvian armies to Siamese jewels to Negro singers. And opium in Africa, eh? You will make your list, everything you require. But first you must come for a look at my gardens. I think you will be impressed. An expense, to be sure, but of what use is money but for the provision of comfort and beauty? Come.'

*   *   *

I remained with Abel Vaudois for two more days while his men picked up the Land Rover and the other tools of the lepidopterist's trade. Abel even thought to include a half dozen beautifully preserved specimens of local butterflies, each neatly mounted in a glass frame. I took the net into the garden and practiced catching various flying insects. I let them all go and after I'd done some damage to a clump of late-blooming hyacinth, I gave up insect-hunting in the garden.

Finally I left in the hours just before dawn, picking up the main highway north from Bangkok. The first stretch of road was broad and flat, with endless stretches of rice fields on either side. The road was built up high because during the rainy season the lands were frequently under water. Even with the height of the road it was occasionally impassable.

When the road got worse, I began to go into my act. I stopped in the small villages and bought my meals from the people, bartering silver coins for crudely spiced bowls of rice and meat. My equipment drew considerable interest, and the villagers were amused that someone would be foolish enough to spend time and money pursuing the pretty little butterflies. I redeemed myself in their eyes by explaining that I sold the insects at a handsome profit to rich collectors—thus it was these rich collectors who were the fools, and I was merely a shrewd tradesman. I would sit cross-legged around village campfires and show the tools of my trade and pass around the half-dozen mounted butterflies for everyone's rapt inspection. I hadn't yet bothered catching any butterflies of my own.

It was at one of these villages, far north of Bangkok, where the rice fields were more and more frequently giving way to stretches of bamboo forest and stands of teak, and where a few coins had bought me a water buffalo steak pounded by hand and rubbed with ginger and broiled over a wood fire, with a spicy root wine to wash it down, that I first began to feel genuinely at ease. In the distance were the noises of the night-time wilderness—monkeys chattering in the trees, the far-off growl of a jungle cat after its prey, the hooting of an owl. And all around me were the soft voices of the local peasantry, *its country's pride*, according to Goldsmith, which *when once destroyed can never be supplied*.

Here the soft voices spoke Siamese. But for the language and the food I could have been almost anywhere—on a hill in Macedonia where my son, Todor, lived, alongside a jungle stream in the Amazon Basin, in a green valley in Slovenia, anywhere. Here Bangkok and Manhattan were equally far removed, light-centuries away. Here people grew their own food and slaughtered their own animals and built their own huts and made their own music and drew their own pictures. Here there were no newspapers, no radios, no jukeboxes, no air conditioning, no central heating, no deodorants, none of the conveniences of modern civilization.

And here, too, I had my first word of

Tuppence. Why, yes, an old woman told me, she had seen some people with black skins, a woman and some men as well. It was remarkable, she had not known there were persons in the world of such a color. They had passed through the village a day after Prang's buffalo had calved, just nine days ago.

They were with the bandits, a man added. But he did not think they were of the bandits but were perhaps their prisoners.

'Bandits? Were they Communists?'

'What are Communists?'

I took a different tack. 'How did you know that the captors of the black persons were bandits?'

'They took food,' the old woman said, 'and did not pay for it, and pointed guns at us. Since they did not have uniforms, we knew they were not of the government, so they must be bandits.'

'Do bandits come here often?'

'Not too often. Farther north there are more bandits, and they are cruel to the villagers. But here only once in a great while do the bandits come to steal from us, and from time to time the soldiers of the government come north looking for bandits, and they too steal from us. But for the most part we are left alone, safe from soldiers and bandits, and we prosper.'

I learned more of the bandits as I moved to the north. There were many groups of them, I

72

was told, and sometimes they fought among themselves and other times they battled the government forces. The bandits hated the government, I learned, and the government had vowed to exterminate the bandits, and it was the peasants who suffered most, as is usually the case. Often the bandits would raid a village and behead the chief of the village and force the young men to go off with them. And if a village chieftain cooperated with the bandits, then the government troops might raid the village and take the young men off to join the army, and the chieftain who had cooperated with the bandits would be shot by an army firing squad. The government had announced that some day all the bandits would be dead, and the bandits had announced that the government would be destroyed and the land would belong to the people, and the villagers sincerely hoped that some day all of the soldiers and all of the bandits would succeed in killing one another.

I heard scattered reports of Tuppence, nothing too certain but bits and pieces picked up here and there. I left the main road and took a road that was not main at all, and only the engineering marvel that was the Land Rover enabled me to keep on going.

Until at last one fine day I emerged in a clearing and suddenly found the Land Rover utterly surrounded by armed men. They were not in uniforms, so I knew they were not government soldiers and guessed that I had found some bandits.

I spoke to them in Siamese; I spoke to them in Khmer. They did not answer. And the next thing I knew I had been stripped naked, divested of clothing and socks and shoes and money belt, and tucked unceremoniously into that horrible bamboo cage.

Now, according to the only bandit who had deigned to talk to me, they were finally ready to kill me.

CHAPTER SIX

The forest began to come awake about half an hour before sunrise. The sky turned from black to gray, and early birds set off in full-throated pursuit of early worms. I crouched in my bamboo home and waited for the bandit camp to wake up. I was beset by the sort of nervous impatience of a toothache victim in a dentist's waiting room, anxious to relieve one pain but a little apprehensive of a greater agony.

They planned to sever my head from my body. I wondered if my head would talk to them after it had been removed—there were cases like that on record, a sort of switch on decapitated chickens racing around barnyards. I seemed to recall that a saint had done

74

something of the sort, blessing those who had effected his martyrdom. I did not expect to bless anyone.

The sun rose, and the little camp came awake. I wondered if Dhang had been able to carry out the final tasks I had assigned to him. I had not seen him in over an hour. He had performed well enough as far as I knew, managing to fetch things from the Land Rover. I now shared my cage with a jar of acid from the car's battery, the insect-killing jar, and a short black bayonet liberated from a sleeping guerrilla. I would have preferred one of their machine pistols, but Dhang had not been able to get one for me; I don't think it would have fit through the bottom of the cage, anyway. I looked at the bayonet, the killing jar, the acid. Then I closed my eyes. One had to work with the materials at hand, but it certainly would have helped to have some more impressive materials available.

A voice rose above the hubbub of the camp and began issuing commands. I watched through the side of the cage as a barefoot young man climbed furiously up the tree from which my cage was suspended. He walked up the trunk as easily as if it had been lying extended upon the ground, then swung out upon the branch. His weight bowed the branch, and the cage dipped toward the ground. Guerrillas moved to surround it. The Thai up in the tree cut the rope, and ten pairs of hands gripped the cage and lowered it gently to the ground.

Another command. Hands unhooked the top of the cage and lifted it up and off. I scooped up the bayonet, the killing jar, and the acid. I got to my feet for the first time since I had first been placed in that unholy prison. My captors gathered around, peering at me over the sides of the cage. They seemed astonished that I had any possessions with me, and one, evidently the commander, demanded to know what these things were that I held.

I scanned the crowd, looking for Dhang. Some twenty guerrillas were clustered close around me, with about as many lounging in the circle of ramshackle huts. Most of them wore panungs, simple pieces of drab cloth wrapped around their small bodies, but here and there I could see various articles of my own clothing.

'What have you? How did you get those things?'

'It is a magic trick,' I said. 'I am a worker of magic and would provide you with entertainment.'

Some of the younger guerrillas began to chatter excitedly. The camp wasn't exactly a major draw on the Orpheum Circuit, and entertainment of any sort was a rare treat. They didn't even get to watch the touring USO shows.

But the leader wasn't having any. 'A bayonet,' he said. 'Where did you get that?'

'By a magic entreaty to my gods.'

'Give me the bayonet.'

If they had only left me my clothes, I could have hidden the bayonet in a trouser leg or something. I looked at him and at the bayonet and wanted to give it to him between the eyes. I glanced past the bunch of guerrillas clustered around me and caught sight of Dhang hovering beside one of the huts. He smiled tentatively and made a sign with his hand to indicate that everything was all right. I was glad he thought so. I nodded briefly to him and handed the bayonet to the chieftain.

Well, I was doing beautifully, I thought. So far I had managed to give up my chief weapon.

'Come out of the cage.'

I couldn't climb over the four-foot cage side without spilling the acid. I gave the killing jar to one of the guerrillas and the jar of acid to another, asked them to hold my magic goods for a moment, and then vaulted the side of the cage. I reclaimed the two jars and began babbling about my prowess as a conjurer and sorcerer. The chief remained unimpressed, but I was earning points with the younger element.

In the center of the camp a broad section of tree trunk rested upon the ground. The top of it was scarred with ax marks and stained with blood. Beside it stood a fat man stripped to the waist, with a massive ax in his hand.

'Go that way,' the chief said, pointing at the man, the ax, the chopping block.

'But the magic—'

'Go.'

The guerrillas moved aside to open a path for me. I walked down it very slowly toward the appointed place of execution. I wondered if Dhang had obtained enough gasoline from the Land Rover. It was impossible for me to teach him how to siphon it, so I had explained how to locate the gas tank from below and told him to puncture it with a bayonet and drain the gasoline from it. He was bright enough, but mechanical tasks were a bit of a puzzle for him, and gasoline was an unknown element. By now it might all have evaporated. And even if it hadn't, he might not put it to the proper use.

And even if he did, it might not work . . .

'Hurry!'

'Sacred Leader,' I intoned. I bowed my head, paused at the execution site. 'Sacred Leader, through a grave misunderstanding you have determined to put me to death. I beg one last request to entertain you with magical visions. If my entertainment does not please you, then I will go willingly to my death.'

'It is an imperialist trick.'

'But will you not observe it, O Leader?'

He truly was interested in nothing but seeing my head say good-bye to my body, but the rest of the group pressured him into it. He stepped back, slapped at the machine pistol on his hip, spat at the ground, sighed, and ordered me to get this foolishness over with as quickly as possible. I knelt by the side of the chopping block and unscrewed the cover of the cyanide jar. I took a deep breath.

'Come close,' I commanded. 'Gather around and breathe deeply of the perfumes of life.'

They gathered around. I let them come as close as they could, and I took a deep breath of my own and held it, and then I poured the cyanide crystals into the jar of battery acid.

I held my breath.

They didn't.

And at that happy moment, just as a dozen of them breathed deeply of the sweet perfume of bitter almonds, Dhang picked up his cue. All at once half a dozen huts burst into flame as the gasoline did its work. Blue-faced guerrillas dropped around me, their lungs filled with cyanide gas. All around the encampment screams burst forth as men fled the burning huts. The chieftain spun around to look at the huts, turned again to look at his men falling like flies. He grabbed at his pistol. I kicked him in the stomach and chopped at the side of his neck and took the pistol away from him.

Across the way a young guerrilla fired wildly at me with a rifle. I saw Dhang loop the butterfly net around his head and knock him off balance. Another man, cursing hysterically, approached Dhang with a machete. I cut him down with a burst from the machine pistol, then spun around to spray a burst of shots at another batch of little men. The pistol was a jerry-built affair; after I'd fired the second burst, it was too hot to hold on to. I threw it aside and snatched up a machete. The fat man, the executioner, came at me with his ax. He swung and missed, and I flailed at him with the machete. It sliced halfway through his throat.

It's hard to say just what happened after that. Dhang was off to one side, taking potshots at his erstwhile comrades with the rifle. I was in the middle of everything, swinging the machete at anyone who got particularly close to me. Around us the fire had spread to all of the huts, encircling the camp in a solid perimeter of fire. Evidently one of the huts was used to store explosives, and when the fire reached it, everything went off at once. That did it, as far as the remaining guerrillas were concerned. I guess they had had enough of magic, especially the sort of sorcery that made smells that put men to sleep and caused huts to explode with the force of an earthquake. They scattered like dandelion seeds in a hurricane, racing through the circle of fire and out into the comparative safety of the jungle.

I went to Dhang. He clapped his hands jubilantly and swung into a mad dance of triumph. 'We have destroyed them,' he shouted. 'Like a thunderbolt from the heavens we have destroyed them, and I shall have a woman. And how the flames shot from the huts! And how the magic gases ate at their vitals! And how the hut was torn by explosions! And how they ran in terror!'

'We'd better get out of here,' I said.

'How they ran! How they screamed!'

'I'll need some clothing. Shoes, anyway. And I can wrap up in a panung, I suppose.' I didn't especially want to strip corpses to get my own clothes back. I took a panung from one of the cyanosed guerrillas and wrapped it around my body, tucking the ends into place. I did manage to find a pair of my own shoes and put them on. They were not particularly comfortable without socks, but it was better than hobbling barefoot through the jungle.

'We will go to the south now?'

'No,' I told Dhang. 'To the north.'

'The north? But more bandits wait in the north. Why shall we go to the north?'

'There is a woman there, and—'

'Ah, that is different,' he said. 'That is good, that is wonderful. If there is a woman there, then that is where we shall go. Of course we will take the rubber-footed buffalo of iron.'

'I'm afraid not.'

He looked at me. 'No? We leave it here?'

'I think it's dead.'

'I killed it? It died when I cut open its stomach?'

The Land Rover had a hole in its gas tank,

and its battery was gone. 'It is dead,' I agreed.

'I did not wish to kill it.'

'It was necessary.'

'I regret it,' he said. 'It is one thing to kill men, but to slaughter such a useful creature—'

'Let's have a look at it,' I said. 'Perhaps we can eat its flesh and make robes of its hide.'

'I do not understand.'

'Let's have a look at the car. Perhaps we can salvage something.'

'Oh.'

CHAPTER SEVEN

'Yevan!'

I turned. 'Not Yevan,' I said, patiently. 'Evan.' Siamese has no words beginning with open vowel sounds, and Dhang had so far prefaced my name with several consonants. 'Evan,' I repeated slowly so that he could watch the way my mouth worked. 'Evan.'

'Heaven.'

'That's better. Evan.'

'Evan.'

'Perfect.'

'Evan—'

'We can continue now.' I turned again, and he yelped my name once more, and I spun around. 'What is it?'

'Do not walk further. That is a trap for

leopards.'

'Where?'

With the tip of his rifle Dhang poked at the ground in front of me. Magically it opened up before him. He brushed aside a network of branches and vines artfully covered with leaves and straw. Below, at the bottom of a six-foot pit, sharpened stakes stood at attention.

'Oh,' I said.

'You must keep sharp eyes. If one were to fall within—'

'Yes.'

'Shall I walk ahead?'

'Perhaps you'd better.'

The narrow jungle roads had been difficult enough even in a Land Rover, but they were ever so much more tedious on foot. It was late afternoon now. We had been walking for what seemed like forever, and were making very little discernible progress. We would have made considerably less progress if I had fallen into a leopard trap.

This was not the first time Dhang had proved useful. Earlier he had whacked the head off a snake with a neat flick of his machete just as the snake had prepared to assault my ankle. And another time, with the sun high in the sky, he had paused to scurry up a tree from which he had tossed down an excellent mangolike fruit. I hadn't realized how hungry I was. The fruit was a welcome change from wormy rice, and we feasted on it.

We were reasonably well equipped for a trek through the jungle. From the guerrilla camp Dhang and I had each taken a machete and a canteen of water. He had a rifle and I had a machine pistol with a full clip in it. The car had yielded up a few treasures, including my flashlight, which the guerrillas had discarded when it failed to operate.

So our equipment was sufficient unto our needs, and Dhang, who was miraculously able to distinguish between jungle trails that led somewhere and jungle trails that did not, and who kept a sharp eye open for leopard traps and pit vipers, was a more than competent guide. Even so, I was a long time shaking the sensation of being in the wrong place. The little village campfires in the rice-growing Thai midlands had been friendly places, places of ease and contentment. The jungle was different. It was dense, it was overgrown, it was blindingly green, and it was alive with any number of animals that emitted menacing noises, some from far away, others too close for anything resembling comfort. I was a long time shaking the feeling that I was in an area that had very obviously not been designed for man's habitation, a hostile environment through which one ought to make one's way as rapidly and guardedly as possible.

And this, of course, was the wrong way to travel. A traveler ought to merge with the landscape through which he moves, becoming as one with his surroundings, rendering the actual process of the journey as effortless as Zen archery. Man, I have found, is a surprisingly adaptable creature; he may have any number of homes, being wholly at home in each in turn as the occasion demands it. I had lived and traveled in this fashion throughout most of central and eastern Europe and the Middle East, in lands that were worlds apart from 107th Street. I had slipped across borders, leaving one language on one side and picking up a new tongue on the other. I had found all of this somewhat easier than I had suspected it might be. But the jungle was a new world, one I had evidently not known in any prior incarnations. I wanted only to fumble through this endless haystack of jungle as quickly as possible, locating a needle named Tuppence and returning posthaste to civilization.

The first night, Dhang shot three small animals and skinned them while I got a fire going. The creatures were built somewhat like rabbits but had small ears and less powerful hind legs. Dhang hacked them into pieces the size of chicken legs, and we cut green sticks from a tree and roasted the meat en brochette. The meat was lean, with a close grain. The slight gamey taste was not at all objectionable. We demolished all three of the little animals. I wondered what they were and if we would be able to get more of them some other time.

I sat cross-legged on the ground. Dhang was busy foraging for more dry wood. He walked along in a half-crouch, stopping now and then to scoop up a fallen twig or branch. He came back with an armload of wood and set it down a few paces from the fire.

'We must keep the fire burning all night,' he said. 'It will keep animals away, and bad spirits.'

'Can't we go any further tonight?'

'It is not good to travel at night. Evil spirits abound. And leopards, which hunt at night. And one can see nothing, and the great owls hoot in the tops of the trees and bats fly. The earth opens beneath one's feet, the sky falls down in a clap of thunder, and the world is evil and dangerous. At night the wise man stays in his hut.'

'But we do not have a hut.'

'We have no hut, Heaven, so we remain by our fire. Here.'

'What's this?'

'Betel. Chew it, and your sleep will be better.'

'What does it do?'

'It improves sleep, and it flushes the worms from one's intestines.'

'Sleep is of no importance to me,' I said, 'and I have no worms in my intestines.'

'Oh.'

'And does it not blacken the teeth?'

'It does, yes.' He looked hurt. 'You do not

86

wish betel, then?'

I thought for a moment. Among its other properties, betel nut contains some substance with a mild narcotic effect, and it occurred to me that such an effect might be a help through the long night. Then, too, there was the When-In-Rome aspect—if I wanted to fit into my surroundings, I might as well chew betel nut like everyone else. I couldn't shrink in size or change my skin color or the shape of my eyes, but I could at least have blackened teeth.

And as far as the intestinal worms were concerned, well who was I to decry the vermifugal properties of betel? I thought of the bowls of wormy rice I had recently ingested. I imagined the effect they might now be having upon my alimentary canal. And, with words of gratitude, I accepted the proffered slice of betel nut.

The betel nut is the heart of the fruit of the areca palm, boiled, sliced, dried, and wrapped up in a leaf of the betel vine. Dhang handed me such a leaf-wrapped slice, and I popped it into my mouth and chewed. It had been flavored with turmeric and cardamom; underneath this flavoring, the nut itself had a slightly bitter taste. I chewed it like a stick of spearmint, and my mouth was suddenly overflowing with saliva. I spat, and the saliva was a deep ruby red. For a terrible moment I thought I was bleeding to death. Then I realized that a rich flow of ruby saliva was a by-product of betel chewing and no cause for alarm.

Beside me Dhang chewed solemnly on another piece of betel, sighed, spat, closed his eyes, and resumed chewing. I fed the fire with scraps of the wood he had collected. It was very dry and burned with little smoke. I chewed and spat and chewed and spat.

'Soon we will reach the village,' Dhang said.

'The village?'

'Tomorrow or the day after. A village in the north country where they may know of your friends. It is not a camp of bandits but a village that lives at peace. The young men from the village join the bandits, but the others are not molested. Perhaps they will have word for us.'

'Why did you join the guerrillas, Dhang?'

He looked intently at me, then arced a stream of red saliva at the fire. It hit the mark and hissed. 'They told me to come,' he said, 'and I went.'

'They forced you to go?'

'Not force.' He considered. 'They said there would be food, and all of us would be together as brothers.' *Chew. Spit.* 'There was nothing of interest in my village. They said that if I went with them, I would be issued a rifle. I had never had a rifle and could not get one in my village.' *Chew.* 'I thought perhaps'—*Spit.*— 'that there might be women. My village was small, and of the women in it many were my cousins and sisters. I have never had a woman.

88

Never. I thought perhaps with the bandits—
but no, nothing. It was very disturbing.'

I shifted the wad of betel nut to the other
side of my mouth. I chewed and spat. The
bitter taste had become rather pleasant by
now. When I was a boy I chewed tobacco once
and, as I recall, vomited. I decided now that
betel was certainly superior to tobacco. I could
see, in fact, how people could get accustomed
to it. I was already feeling oddly at peace with
the world around me. *Chew.* The sense of
surrounding hostility was easing up. *Spit.* The
tension was going away. I kicked off my shoes
and wiggled my toes. I watched the flames
dancing in the fire.

We went on talking, Dhang and I. He was, I
guess, about nineteen or twenty years old,
though he did not know his age in years. He
had lived all his life in the jungles of the north
and knew virtually nothing about the world
around him. He could not read or write. He
had no political orientation whatsoever and
did not know whether the bandits were
Communists or not because he did not know
what Communists were. He knew there was a
king in Bangkok, and that the king had many
soldiers, and that the bandits and the king's
soldiers were sworn enemies. He had been
told that when all of the king's soldiers were
dead, there would be rice and fruit for all of
the people in the land, and on that day the
bandits would become the leaders of all the

people. Whether or not such a situation would be good did not seem to have occurred to him. Good and bad, in Dhang's frame of reference, seemed to be largely subjective; such a turn of events would be demonstrably good for the bandits, just as it would be bad for the soldiers of the king.

Politically unsophisticated as he was, Dhang found my own motives perfectly sensible. A girl who was my friend and lover was held prisoner by bandits, so I would go to rescue her. That was logical, because friends took care of one another and loved one another and sacrificed themselves for one another, because that was the whole purpose of friendship. By the same token, Dhang and I were friends and would strive to keep one another from harm. And, by extension, he would help me rescue Tuppence, and I in turn would help him find a woman. Such behavior, to Dhang, was eminently justifiable.

But to more knowledgeable men, to men like Barclay Houghton Hewlitt and the Chief, a journey of hazard and hardship demanded a more complex purpose. Barclay Houghton Hewlitt thought I would undertake a trip to Thailand so that my government might be better informed in respect to Thai guerrilla activity. The Chief thought I would hop around the world so that Africans could cut in on the Chinese opium trade. These were motives that they could appreciate and that

90

simple little Dhang would find wholly incomprehensible.

On reflection I decided that I rather preferred his world view.

We talked on, chewing betel and spitting and feeding our little fire, while the night life of the jungle came awake around us. The noises, ominous to me earlier, were now nothing more than jungle music, the pleasant rhythms of life and nature. Dhang sighed, spat out his piece of betel, stretched out on his back, and closed his eyes. I lay down on my side and went on chewing betel nut. My mind wandered, and time slipped gently by, and I chewed and spat and chewed and spat.

I suppose I dreamed. I didn't sleep, but exhaustion and the narcotic agent of the betel nut combined to produce something that could only be categorized as a dream. My mind slipped into new channels, part memory and part fantasy. I had long, silent conversations with myself. I closed my eyes and let an endless parade of images play through my mind like a surrealistic movie. It lasted for quite a while. At any time I could have stopped the dream by opening my eyes and sitting up, but the dream was pleasant, and I more or less controlled it, as one is said to be able to do when smoking opium. Eventually I did sit up and open my eyes and spit out the remains of the betel nut, and the dream went away, and I waited for the sun to rise and for Dhang to wake up.

*   *   *

We spent the following night by the side of a swiftly flowing stream. We caught several small fishes, dug a hole, wrapped the fish in wet leaves, then put them in the hole and covered them with a layer of earth. We built our fire on top of them and let it burn for a long time. The fish baked beneath the fire, and when we pushed it aside and dug them up, they were perfectly cooked, tender and flaky and delicious. We ate well and talked of women, and then Dhang slept while I treated myself to another betel-inspired dream.

By now our conversations were devoted almost entirely to sex. Dhang would say, 'Tell me about the women, Evan,' and I would feel like George telling Lennie about the rabbits. But I would talk, and he would listen intently, interrupting now and then with a question.

Dhang's original approach to lovemaking was only slightly less primitive than the jungle around us. As he understood it, one located a woman, threw her down on the ground, removed her panung, kneed her in the stomach until she opened her legs, and then raped her. If one had a wife, of course, matters could be more simply managed; then one's woman submitted voluntarily to rape, and force was unnecessary.

The concept of mutual cooperation in lovemaking was a new one to Dhang. At first he didn't know what to make of it and was not certain whether or not I was telling the truth. For a while I felt like a Peace Corps worker explaining the American governmental system to a Borneo tribesman—at first my listener thought the whole business was unnecessarily complex and then he began to realize its infinite possibilities.

So I taught him as much as I could, given the circumstantial limitations. One of these was language. While my command of Siamese was fairly good, there were certain words that simply do not turn up on Linguaphone records. I made do by teaching Dhang the English equivalents. He had the excellent verbal memory of the illiterate; when one cannot rely on reading and writing, and when one's mind is generally uncluttered with excess facts, one learns to remember what one hears. So Dhang learned the English words for the more interesting parts of the body and the functions they performed, and, since it seemed unlikely that he would ever have to worry about conducting himself properly in polite English-speaking society, I didn't bother teaching him euphemisms. Instead I taught him good old four-letter words.

Of course there was another handicap. For the time being, as long as we were stuck off in the jungle, his education was hopelessly academic. It was a little like learning to swim in the middle of the Sahara desert. On the theory that a picture was worth a thousand words, I scratched occasional pornographic graffiti in the earth with the tip of the machete. But a live model would have been worth at least a thousand pictures, and I had the feeling that, unless we found one soon, Dhang would begin frothing at the mouth.

Still, he slept well that night. Perhaps the betel nut helped. By the time he awoke the next morning, I had caught fresh fish for breakfast. We ate, washed ourselves in the stream, and pushed onward. For a stretch the jungle trail was overgrown to the point of impenetrability, and we had to hack our way through a dense cover of vines and shrubbery. But eventually the growth thinned out, and we made fairly good time again. By midafternoon we reached a large clearing in the jungle, the village Dhang had told me about. Some forty huts were pitched around the perimeter of the clearing. In the center all manner of activity was going on. A youth was carefully slitting the throat of a buffalo calf, a trio of old women were washing clothes, and another woman was grinding rice to paste for the preparation of rice cakes. The village came to life at our appearance, with men emerging from the huts, most of them armed with spears or machetes.

Siamese was not spoken here. Dhang talked with one of the village leaders in a dialect of

Khmer. I could not follow the conversation completely but managed to catch the gist of it. Dhang explained that we came in peace, that we were not bandits, that we had destroyed a bandit camp to the south and were forced to flee for our lives. This won us a good deal of sympathy. He went on to tell how we were attempting to rescue some black persons who had been recently captured by the bandits. If we could enjoy the hospitality of the village for the night and if we could be informed about the black people whom the bandits had abducted, we would be eternally grateful and would offer up prayers for the souls of all the villagers.

The chieftain clucked over this and said that he had heard of the black persons and had not believed that they existed. He looked covertly at me and said that he had seen white persons before and thought that they were most unusual, but of course he knew that there were such persons. He had never known that there were black persons, however. Yet he had heard of black persons only recently and he would be glad to summon the villagers together to find out what was known about them. But in the meantime he suggested we relax and sample the hospitality his humble village could provide. As we could see, he said, it was an evening of feasting; they had slaughtered a calf to celebrate the first night of the Week of Tears and Sighs, which commemorated the

95

death by fire of the infant sons and daughters of the gods. There would be meat for all that evening, and speeches and singing, and rice cakes and betel nut, and it would honor them that we might participate in their celebration.

'Feasting,' Dhang said, translating for me. 'And women, one can see that this village overflows with women. Look at that one!'

He pointed at a plump young girl, perhaps sixteen years old, her panung covering her primly from her ankles to her waist, her lovely yellow-brown breasts peering out between silky strands of jet black hair. She looked our way, stared, then giggled musically and ran away. For a moment I thought Dhang might run after her, but he somehow managed to control himself.

'You will abandon me,' I said to him. 'You will enjoy the embrace of one of these women and you will not assist me with my search.'

'That is not true, Heaven,' he said. He still had trouble with my name, but he got it right about half the time. 'That is not true. You know that I am your friend and that I have sworn to come with you.'

'I treasure your friendship, Dhang.'

'But perhaps we can linger in this village for an extra day. It would not mean so much, a single day. A day to exhaust ourselves with the women, and then we can continue with the search.'

It seemed reasonable enough. The village

chief had evidently decided that our coming on the feast day was providential, and that we were thus to be considered guests of honor. In that capacity it stood to reason that Dhang would be furnished with female companionship for the evening. With two nights and a day to sow wild rice, he would be able to travel again and would be unhampered by the frustration that was currently knotting him up.

Of course, if he ran true to form, he would be as intent upon talking about what he had done as he now was upon talking about what he had not done. But that would at least provide a refreshing change of pace.

'We will stay,' I said, 'until the morning after tomorrow morning.'

'I am grateful, Evan.'

For the remainder of the afternoon we had the run of the village. I exchanged my panung, which had grown rather filthy, for a clean one. A villager admired my American shoes. After a couple days of walking sockless through the jungle my own admiration for the shoes was considerably qualified, and I was happy to exchange them for a pair of open sandals. I knew enough Khmer to carry on rudimentary conversations and as I wandered around the village I got the hang of the particular dialect they spoke there. I wasn't exactly fluent in it, but I could make myself understood and could occasionally understand the replies to my questions.

No one had the whole story on Tuppence and the quartet. No one had actually sighted them, but various villagers had been subjected to various rumors from men of other villages and other tribes, and the result of collating different bits of data was something like this— four black men and one black girl had been held captive by a band of notorious bandits. The bandits were not of this immediate region, but had come from the northwest, evidently in Laos. They had stolen down through the Thai jungles to make their capture and were now returning from whence they came.

Curiouser and curiouser, I thought. A kidnapping by Thai guerrillas made a certain amount of sense; Tuppence and the musicians could be used as pawns in some maneuvering between the guerrillas and the Bangkok regime. But why would the Laotians be interested in snatching a quintet of visiting Americans? I couldn't figure it out.

I was still puzzling it out when the feast began. The slaughtered calf was run through with a spit and roasted over a roaring fire in the center of the clearing. The entire population of the village sat in a circle around the fire. As guests of honor, Dhang and I received one eye and half of the calf's brains, along with a couple of rice cakes and some vegetable stew. Dhang seemed to enjoy his food. I had never tasted anything so profoundly revolting in my life. I ate everything that was given to me, as a proper guest of honor should, and at the conclusion of the meal I wandered off into the jungle, far out of hearing range, and spent some twenty minutes vomiting.

I returned to the village. Everyone seemed to be having a marvelous time. On one side a storyteller was amusing a gathering of children. Across the way a crowd of men and women sang and danced beside the fire. An old man sat on his haunches, playing odd music on a hollow reed.

And Dhang had gone off with the first girl he had pointed out, the plump little topless one. I saw the two of them in the doorway of one of the huts.

'You and I,' he said in Khmer, 'phuck,' he said in English. 'Purick in cunat.' He cupped her breast, stroked it, kissed her mouth. She seemed puzzled. He undid her panung and pulled it off, and he divested himself of his own panung, and he rolled on top of her, and she rolled out from under him and screamed, and all hell broke loose.

The elders of the village immediately surrounded him. The girl was led away by an old woman, and the men pointed their spears at Dhang and seemed prepared to kill him at once. I ran through the crowd to his side. He stood with his mouth hanging open, naked, defenseless, his only weapon a spear designed for another sort of combat entirely.

'So this is how you repay hospitality,' the old chief said scornfully. 'You gorge yourself upon eyes and brains and do thus in return. We treat you as emissaries from the gods, and you behave as devils.'

Dhang was babbling that he had never had a girl and would die if he did not get one soon. It looked as though he might die regardless. All around us voices rose up in anger. I tried to get through to the chief, but I had trouble making out what he was saying. Perhaps the girl was a priestess, I thought, or someone else's wife, or something of the sort. But why should that so profoundly disturb the entire village?

It was Dhang who explained it to me. After they had sent us on our way, after they had taken us to the edge of the clearing and ordered us to walk off into the night, Dhang translated it all for me.

'It is not permitted,' he said. 'Throughout the entire Week of Tears and Sighs sexual relations of any sort are forbidden under penalty of death. If we had come at any other time, we could have had any woman in the village. Any one at all, we would have only to choose. Any of them—'

His voice broke. We walked through utter darkness in utter silence. I tripped on a vine and said one of the English words I had taught him.

'I wanted to,' he said. 'But it was forbidden. I touched her. Her tit. How soft and smooth. She had a delicious smell. She was warm. She would have let me have her but for the custom. I took off her panung, I saw all of her body . . .'

We walked onward.

'I ache,' he said. He touched himself. 'I am in pain.'

'Chew some betel.'

He popped a slice of betel nut into his mouth. His jaws worked furiously, and he spat.

'I still ache,' he said.

'I was afraid of that.'

'If they had waited just a few minutes, Evan! I actually touched her cunat with my purick. In another moment—'

'Don't think about it.'

'But how can I avoid thinking about it?'

He fell silent. We trudged on a few more paces, then gave it up; it was impossible to see clearly and seemed pointless to continue stumbling about in the darkness. I had a few matches left and managed to light a small fire of leaves and twigs.

'I will not be able to sleep,' he said.

'You will sleep.'

'We could go back in a week, when the Week of Tears and Sighs is ended. Perhaps I could have her then.'

'Perhaps.'

'No. They think we are devils now. They say that we are barbarians. I shall never have that

101

girl, Evan.'

'There are other girls.'

'Ah,' he said. 'But where?'

CHAPTER EIGHT

Crossing the border from Thailand to Laos is about as awe-inspiring an experience as crossing from Connecticut to Rhode Island. When you go into Rhode Island, at least there's a sign that welcomes you to the state and tells you what the speed limit is and all the terrible things that will happen to you if you exceed it. And you know exactly when you cross that border, too; the surface of the road changes to show you where the Connecticut road crew stopped paving and where the Rhode Island crew took over. None of those formalities are observed when you sneak across from Thailand to Laos. One morning we were in Thailand and that afternoon we were in Laos, and somewhere along the way there had been a border that we had crossed, but the exact moment of our crossing remains undetermined.

We had come a long way, Dhang and I, and it had been an equally frustrating journey for both of us, albeit for different reasons. Dhang was still a virgin, and I was still uncertain as to Tuppence's whereabouts, or whether she was alive or dead, or precisely why she had been kidnapped in the first place. We had met occasional natives who had heard occasional rumors that pointed us down a particular jungle trail in pursuit of the four black men and one black woman, but I had been no more successful in getting precise information from the natives than had Dhang in finding a woman.

We had made progress of a sort. We had moved from a portion of Thailand that was vaguely and ineffectually dominated by vaguely Communist-oriented guerrillas to a portion of Laos that was quite thoroughly controlled by the forces of the Communist Pathet Lao. We had, in other words, successfully worked our way out of the frying pan and into the fire, had wriggled off the spit and dropped into the coals.

We kept moving. The jungle thinned out and gave way to level land with a scattering of trees here and there. At a river bank we stopped to drink and wash ourselves. A stranger looked back at me from the water's surface. I had not shaved since leaving Bangkok, and my beard was thick and wild. The sun had done a good job on the unbearded portions of my face, and the betel nuts that I had been chewing more and more frequently of late had turned my teeth quite black. I did not look much like myself, but neither did I look like someone indigenous to the region. I looked as though I ought to be lurking on a mountain in Bhutan or Nepal waiting to terrify passersby. There was no snow around, but I certainly looked and felt abominable.

We pressed onward across the plateau and into the craggy, mountainous country. The path widened into a rude sort of road, and a few miles further on, the road was paved after a fashion with loose gravel. We stopped at a roadside hut to ask directions to the nearest town. The woman who answered our knock looked at our weapons and my beard and shrank in terror. Dhang explained calmly that we came in peace, that we were holy men, that we wished to know the route to the nearest town. She told us haltingly to follow the road for about an hour's time to the city of Tao Dan.

'Too old,' Dhang said.

'What?'

'The woman. She was too old, and her skin was wrinkled.'

'There will be younger women.'

'Perhaps,' he said, and fell silent.

We walked for what seemed like a good deal more than an hour until, from the top of a hill, we saw the town of Tao Dan in the distance. It was a fairly sizable city, a great change from the hut-encircled jungle villages we had passed through. A town of that size meant policemen and sundry officials, which in turn meant that I would draw an uncomfortable amount of attention. It was unsafe to go there, but at the same time the town seemed the most logical place to get word of Tuppence.

We walked about halfway there. Then I took Dhang by the arm. 'Leave your weapons with me,' I told him. 'I'll wait out of sight in the brush. Go to the town and make inquiries. Say merely that you are a Thai and have made a journey from the west. Say that you have heard that black men and a black woman were to be seen in the area and see what you can find out about them.'

'And you will wait here?'

'Yes. Find out as much as you can, then come back here. You will be able to learn more now, when people are awake. Try to obtain clothing for yourself, and for me if it is possible. At night, when all is dark, then we will both be able to pass safely through the town.'

'You will wait for me, Heaven?'

'Yes.'

'If the police ask me who I am—'

'Tell them your name and your village, that is all. Do not tell them about me.'

'I will not.'

'Good.'

'Evan? How will I obtain clothing? Or food?'

'You have no money?'

He shook his head. I had no money, either;

the guerrillas had taken my money belt along with everything else, for whatever good it was to them. I still had the flashlight, but the thought of Dhang attempting to pass a British gold sovereign in a provincial Laotian town was somehow disquieting. The only other articles of value in our possession were the rifle, the machine pistol, the machetes, and the canteens. I had the feeling that it would be impossible to exchange the guns for anything. They would simply be confiscated by the authorities. I asked Dhang if he thought he could use the machetes and the canteens for barter, and he said he thought he could.

'I'll keep one canteen, though,' I said. 'I'd hate to run out of water. And you'd better leave me some betel nut.' It was surprising I thought, how quickly habits could develop. 'Be cautious with your questions. Try to attract as little attention as possible, but learn as much as you possibly can. Do you understand?'

'Yes, Evan.'

'Go, now. And return as soon as possible.'

'Yes. Yevan?'

'You're doing it again, you said Yevan. Evan.'

'Evan. If I find a girl in the town . . .'

He looked at me, hope in his eyes. He would not find a girl, I thought, and if he did, she would have nothing to do with him. But it seemed less than kind to tell him this. Nor was there any point in ordering him to come

106

directly back to me without wasting his time on whatever woman he happened to locate. If I told him to, he would still follow his instincts and then might be so dismayed at having disobeyed me that he would desert me altogether. The secret of command, I decided, lies largely in giving orders that are apt to be obeyed.

'If you should find a woman,' I told him, 'may the gods grant you enjoyment. But do not dally too long with her and come back to me when time permits.'

I watched him head on down the road, a machete in either hand, a canteen slung over one shoulder. He did not cut a particularly heroic figure, that little man bobbing along, lost in the immensity of the Laotian landscape. His own self-confidence was at that moment the only confidence he inspired. I had a terrible feeling that I was dispatching him to certain doom, my own doom to follow shortly when he told the Laotian Communists where to find me.

I made myself reasonably comfortable in a clump of brush some twenty yards from the side of the road. I popped a chunk of betel nut into my mouth and chewed and spat and chewed and spat. It was quite possible, I thought, that Tuppence and the four musicians were being held prisoner within Tao Dan itself. From the long-range view I'd had of the city, it seemed likely to be the largest town in the immediate area. If the rumors I had sifted added up as I had added them, the five had been kidnapped by Laotians and taken into Laos. They would probably have wound up on this very road and thus would have passed through Tao Dan. They might well be there now.

If that were the case, the whole village would be aware of their presence. Dhang would learn where they were being kept. He would return before long, and under cover of darkness the two of us would sneak into the city. While Tao Dan slept we would find where Tuppence and the others were being held prisoner. Perhaps there would be a guard or two to overpower. Once that was done, we would liberate the prisoners and escape.

I thought the thing through about that far and then let go of it. The details to follow— just how we would escape and just where we would go and so on—I did not want to think about for the time being. It was simpler by far to sit back comfortably and chew the betel nut.

And then, after a long time of sitting and chewing and spitting, I heard the jeep.

It was just a low rumble at first, like the droning of a persistent insect. Then it came closer, and I recognized the sound as a car of some sort. I had been a long time in the wilderness, and this was the first mechanized vehicle I had heard since the guerrillas had halted my Land Rover. I peered through the underbrush and watched as a U.S. army jeep came into sight at the crest of a hill. For a hysterical moment I thought that I was being rescued by a detachment of Green Berets. Then reality intruded—evidently the vehicle was one that had been captured by the Pathet Lao's troops during the fighting in the Plain of Jars.

The jeep passed me and headed on toward Tao Dan. There were two uniformed soldiers in the front seat and a third in the back. I watched the jeep disappear over the next rise in the road, then listened as the sound of its engine faded and died in the still afternoon air.

I shifted the hunk of betel nut from one side of my mouth to the other. I chewed like a cow munching its cud, then arced a stream of red juice off to the left. I told myself quietly that I should have stayed in New York. With all of its muggings and stabbings and race riots and air pollution, it was worlds safer than the hills of Laos. The FBI agents who bugged my apartment and the CIA clowns who read my mail were nuisances, but they had never done me any appreciable harm.

And at least in New York my life had a sort of purpose. I went to meetings, I sent articles to newspapers and magazines, I ground out theses for inept scholars, and I did what I could to support a wide array of noble lost causes. I made myself useful. Minna depended

109

upon me, and so, in a more remote way, did my son, Todor, in Macedonia. Now Todor's mother, according to word that had made its way from Macedonia to Athens to London to New York, was awaiting another child.

What good would I be to that unborn child or to Todor or to Minna or to anyone if I managed to get myself killed chasing wild geese in Laos?

I chewed. I spat inexpertly, and ruby saliva trickled through my beard. I wiped it away and said one of the English words I had taught Dhang. Somehow the sight of the jeep had brought reality home to me in an uncomfortable way. We were out of the jungle now. We had returned to a mechanized world, a world of cars and planes, of rapid-fire automatic weapons, of uniformed soldiers, of passports and visas and sundry documents. If Tuppence were a prisoner in Tao Dan, she was no doubt a well-guarded prisoner. They were not a band of primitive guerrillas. They would not have her hanging in a bamboo cage. I could not dance naked among the uniformed guards, babbling of magic tricks and gassing them with cyanide. Nor could I expect the town of Tao Dan to lie sleeping when I visited it in the dead of night. There would be men on duty all night long, and one glance at me would assure them that something was wrong, and they would either shoot me or capture me or both.

I uncapped my canteen, took a sip of water, and rubbed the tip of my index finger over my blackened teeth. I stretched out on the ground and closed my eyes and gave myself up to a veritable orgy of betel nut mastication. The narcotic properties of the nut could not begin to cope with the general wave of paranoia that was beginning to engulf me. I divided my thoughts into rumination over what had already gone wrong and speculation as to what would go wrong next. The waking dreams that the betel nut provided were fantasies of terror and betrayal.

Dhang would sell me out, I decided. He had one thing on his mind and one thing only and he would do anything to get what he wanted. After all, one had merely to look at his past performance chart. Once I promised him a woman, he promptly betrayed his guerrilla companions and cheerfully joined me in annihilating them left and right. Now, in Tao Dan, he would stick to form. He would go to the authorities and explain that if they provide him with a woman, he would repay them by leading them straight to an American spy who was conspiring against the Pathet Lao.

I couldn't really trust him, I told myself. For that matter, I couldn't trust anyone.

Tuppence, for example. What did I know about Miss T'pani Ngawa, when you came right down to it?

Blessed little. It had somehow never

occurred to me to wonder whether the kidnapping had been the genuine article. But now that I thought it over, there was more than one possible explanation. Suppose she and the quartet had not been kidnapped at all. Suppose they had managed to steal the royal gems all by themselves, and suppose they had subsequently headed for Laos quite voluntarily, picking the northern retreat as the safest and simplest escape route. Any reason why that was impossible?

None that I could think of. The more I thought it over, the more possible it became. I actually knew rather little of Tuppence's political leanings. Every type of political orientation was represented in Africa lately, and both the far right and the far left were to be found in such organizations as the Pan-African Unity League. Tuppence had given the impression of being generally apolitical, a sharp and fun-loving girl more interested in treble and bass than in left and right. Yet it might all have been a pose.

What if Tuppence had been a Communist all along?

It was possible, I told myself. She could have come to the States as a Communist agent ordered to infiltrate Black Nationalist political groups. Then, when the State Department sent her on a Far Eastern tour, she bided her time and waited for a chance to strike a blow at the West. She masterminded a plot to steal the jewels, thus driving a wedge between the United States and Thailand, and ran off to freedom in Pathet Lao territory in Laos. And then, after she was home free, some hare-brained insomniac named Tanner was fool enough to chase all over Southeast Asia to rescue her.

That would be the best one yet, I thought. Here the knight sets out in shining armor and winds up with his armor severely tarnished and his lance broken and his teeth black and his beard itching murderously; and when he finally approaches the dragon's lair, it develops that the tender maiden has a thing for dragons and wants to stay right where she is.

Beautiful—

Understand, these thoughts did not come all at once. They spaced themselves over the hours, and they were broken up with other interesting observations—that I was getting hungry, that I was tired, that the sky was darkening, that I was very hungry, that I was very tired, that Dhang had evidently disappeared, and, finally, that it was night.

And he still hadn't come back.

The night was cold and dark and damp and gave every appearance of lasting forever. Clouds blotted out the moon and all the stars. I did not really have to remain hidden in the clump of brush. I would have been equally invisible in the middle of the road. It was that dark. After a while I decided that one did not have to be a paranoid to realize that Dhang was not returning for me. If the darkness had not been so utterly impenetrable, I might have tried going on after him, but as things stood, it was out of the question. I hefted the flashlight and clucked at it. At that moment I would have gladly traded it, gold and all, for a flashlight that worked.

There was nothing to do but wait for daylight or for Dhang, whichever appeared first. I curled up in the clump of brush and chewed betel and waited and hoped something would happen, and eventually something did.

It began to rain.

The rain didn't last very long. This was fortunate; a steady downpour like that one would have flooded all of Southeast Asia if it had lasted an hour or so. As it was, it rained on me without interruption for perhaps fifteen minutes, at the conclusion of which time I was soaked through to the bone.

There was nothing to do but sit there like an idiot and get rained on. The ground on which I sat quietly turned itself into a sea of mud. The rain pelted my panung until I thought the poor garment would dissolve. There was no cover available, no place to go, no way to see where I was going if I tried. I stayed where I was and I got very wet, and finally, after a fifteen-minute version of eternity, the rain gave up.

I sat through the rest of the night, shivering, shaking, now and then rending the still night air with a sneeze. I waited for Dhang and for daybreak with the certain feeling that neither would ever arrive. There was nothing to eat. I had run out of betel nut. Everything that could possibly go wrong had already gone wrong, and if someone had come up and shot me, it would have been anti-climactic.

CHAPTER NINE

When dawn broke, finally, I left my weapons and my canteen in the clump of brush and started down the road with the flashlight, a wet, feverish Diogenes with an inoperative lantern. I left the weapons behind because I was fairly certain they wouldn't work anyway after all that rain and mud, and I left the canteen behind because I could not imagine ever wanting water again. I walked off down the road in the general direction of Tao Dan and I stopped at the first hut I saw.

It didn't require any great courage to walk into the little shack. I decided that the worst that could happen was that I would get killed and I told myself reasonably that this was probably also the best thing that could happen. I went inside. An old man sat in a chair that someone had fashioned from an empty oil drum. He was smoking a pipe. He looked wordlessly at me, his eyes saying that he had

115

seen all manner of strangeness in his time, that I admittedly was one of the stranger phenomena to which he had been subjected, but that it would take more than a wet, bearded maniac to rattle his composure.

'I must wash myself and remove my beard,' I said. 'I require dry clothing. And food. I have not eaten in many hours and must have food.'

He merely looked at me.

'I am hungry,' I said. I made pantomime motions, one hand clutching an invisible rice bowl, the other shoveling food into my mouth. 'Food, a shave, clothing—'

'You are not of this country.'

'No, I am not.'

'Parlez-vous français?'

'Oui, je parle français—'

And off we went in French. I don't suppose I should have been surprised. French influence had been considerable in Indochina since 1787, and the French had held the area as a protectorate for many years before Dienbienphu. Still, I had been talking and thinking in nothing but Siamese and Khmer of late, and the sudden transition to an Occidental language was jarring. The old man spoke reasonably good French and seemed delighted at the chance to show it off.

'For years I worked for the French,' he said. 'I was a very valuable man for them. I was chief overseer on a large rubber plantation. They knew that I possessed the ability to keep

116

the native laborers in line. I was well paid and performed my work with skill and diligence.' He turned sad eyes on the mud-floored hut. 'And look at me now,' he said. 'At what I have come to.'

'These are bad times,' I said.

'They are. That a man like myself should not be respected in my old age. The Communists and anarchists run wild throughout the country. Ah, bad times, eh?'

I thought to myself that the old man was lucky to be alive at all. After all the years he had spent serving the French colonial interests, it was incredible that he hadn't been killed after the liberation, even more extraordinary that he was allowed to remain alive in Pathet Lao territory. Yet it was undeniable that his present life was a great comedown from earlier prosperity. The hut contained a straw pallet in one corner, a kerosene stove, a few pots and pans, the oil drum chair, and very little else.

'You are French, my boy?'

'Yes.' My head was reeling. *I am whatever you want me to be*, I thought. *Feed me, clothe me, let me sit by the side of the stove, and I will be any nationality you prefer.*

'From Paris?'

'That is correct.'

'What district? Saint-Germain-des-Prés? Montmartre? Montparnasse? Ah, you are surprised at my knowledge of Paris, are you not? And I will tell you something that will further astonish you. I have never been to the beautiful France. It has been my dream, but I have never been there. I live and die in this wilderness.' He shook his head. 'Once this devastation was a part of France, a part of the French empire. Once it was on the road to dignity, to civilization, to life itself. Now!'

I said, 'Perhaps one day—'

Gallic fire burned in his wrinkled brown face. 'Ah! I can see it now as I have so often seen it in my dreams. *Mon Général* Charles de Gaulle leading battalions of French troops through all of Indochina, recovering lost territory, bringing my poor country back under the protection of the French flag! And at his side those other brave soldiers of the beautiful France . . .'—and he named two generals who had been implicated in an OAS plot to assassinate De Gaulle.

'Perhaps that day will come, old one.'

'That I may live to see it,' he said fervently. 'That I may live to see my poor country take her place among the lands of the French Empire, side by side with France herself, and with Algeria, and Senegal, and French Equatorial Africa, and Quebec—'

I stiffened at attention. I began, thin of voice and oddly lightheaded, to sing the 'Marseillaise.' ' "Allons, enfants de la patrie—" '

He jumped to his feet. ' "*Le jour de gloire est arrivé,*" ' he sang out loud and clear, his hand

118

over his heart.

*   *   *

'To share with you my rice bowl and my razor, that is my pleasure,' the old man was saying. 'But clothing is another matter. My own would not fit you, and I have no other. Perhaps it would be possible to dry your garment by the fire . . .'

My garment was filthy as well as sopping. Besides, I had the feeling that a panung draped around me would render me fairly conspicuous in a town like Tao Dan.

'I have money,' I said.

'I fear the money of France is no longer of use in this land.'

'I have gold.'

'Gold!' His eyes brightened. 'Gold is another matter. No matter who runs a nation, no one is fool enough to despise gold. It is the universal solvent. Everyone softens in its presence. You wish me to purchase clothing for you? To obtain anything of quality I would have to go into town—'

'I don't want quality. Just ordinary peasant clothing.'

'Ah,' he said. He eyed me closely. 'You are French and would pass as a peasant. When one grows old, one asks too many questions. I wonder if you might be working secretly for the French government?'

'Well—'

'Say no more. Perhaps if the day of glory has not arrived, well, perhaps it is not too far away, *hein*? Let me consider. You wish to pass as a peasant, is it so? You are tall for one of us, but that is not so great a difficulty. The Muong tribesmen are men of some height. It is your fair complexion and large white eyes which render you noticeable. In Tao Dan you would be quickly recognized, I fear.'

'Perhaps I could ride in a cart or something. The less anyone sees of me.'

'Ah, yes. If I had a bullock, you could ride in a bullock cart, and fewer men would look upon your face. But I have no bullock.'

'Could you buy one for me?'

'Have you much gold?'

I unscrewed the back of the flashlight and took out the dummy battery. I pried the case open and spilled the gold coins into the palm of my hand. The old man's eyes went wide at the sight of them. It was a shame, I thought, that I had chosen British sovereigns. A roll of Napoleons d'or might have had more impact upon the old Francophile.

But gold, evidently, was gold the world over; it mattered little whether the head on it was that of Louis Napoleon or Victoria Hanover. 'With this it will be a simple matter to purchase a bullock and a cart,' he said. 'And clothing as well. There is more than enough.'

'You may keep whatever is left for yourself.'

'It is not necessary, my friend.'

'France rewards her faithful sons,' I said. Besides, I thought, leaving the rest with him would keep him free from temptation.

'It is reward enough to serve the beautiful France.'

'Would you be in poverty on the day of liberation?'

He lowered his head in gratitude. 'I will be able to buy a mattress,' he said. 'And perhaps a bullock to ease my labor in the fields. I shall not forget this.' He was silent for a moment. Then, quickly, he scooped up the handful of yellow coins. 'I go now,' he said. 'I shall return with clothing and the bullock and cart. My razor, here. There is water, you may heat it upon the stove. I have no soap.'

'I will manage.'

'What food I have is in the pot. You see it? I will bring more food. Good food. Not the *haute cuisine*, I regret, but the best that it is possible to find in this godforsaken land.'

'It would be well,' I suggested, 'that no one know too much about this gold or whence it came.'

'No one will know.' The old eyes narrowed. 'No man will wish to talk, for talk would bring official inquiry, and the officials would confiscate the gold. It is not permitted to own gold here. But the people, the people prefer to retain their gold nevertheless.'

At least the French had taught one lesson, I

121

thought. The French peasantry and the bourgeoisie as well are notorious hoarders of gold and silver, and periodic inflation over the years has proven them right more often than not. I hoped the habit of secret hoarding persisted in Laos.

The old man left. I heated water on the stove and soaked my beard. His ancient straight razor was sharp enough, but it had a particularly difficult job ahead of it. My beard was long enough to be difficult with abundant lather, and shaving it off without any soap at all was quite a problem. I didn't even have a mirror but had to make do with the shiny bottom of a cooking pot, which was more trouble than it was worth. The straight razor is a depressingly barbaric instrument to begin with, and I was not using it under optimum conditions. Still, I managed to get the job done. I accumulated a few minor nicks, scraped myself here and there, and wound up looking like something less than a matinée idol, but at least the beard was gone.

My complexion was still very wrong, the effects of the sun on my forehead notwithstanding. I stuffed a wad of the old man's pipe tobacco into my mouth and chewed it as if it were betel nut. It tasted terrible. I spat tobacco juice into my cupped hands and rubbed it all over my face. It burned in the shaving nicks like white phosphorus— although, come to think of it, it probably functioned as an antiseptic in the process. I checked the mirror surface of the cooking pot and decided that the results were not entirely ineffective. I chewed more tobacco, rubbed the juice on my face, and kept repeating the process until I was satisfied with the yellow-brown color I had achieved.

My big white eyes were another problem. I pulled at the skin just behind the corner of each eye—it produced the desired effect, but I would have had to staple the skin to the bone to maintain it. I experimented with squinting, which didn't work, and with keeping my eyes half lidded, which was a little better.

The whole shape of my head was wrong, but there was nothing much I could do about that. The mouth, though, was the most glaringly bad feature. It was too big, the lips too prominent. I practiced drawing my lips in and making my mouth appear smaller, working both with and without the improvised mirror. This made quite a difference. One of the main reasons why people in different countries look different is that they learn from the cradle to handle their faces in certain ways. By lowering my eyelids and compressing my lips I did not quite manage to look Laotian, but I did succeed in rendering myself somewhat less conspicuous. I might not fool anyone who took a very close look, but maybe, with luck, no one would get that close to me.

A wave of nausea shook me. I went to the

stove and picked up the pot of rice. It had been cooked in some sort of animal fat and was well seasoned. I was ravenous, and it tasted excellent, and even at that I had trouble getting the rice down and even more trouble keeping it down. I felt feverish and weak.

I wondered what had become of Dhang, and I wondered what had happened to Tuppence, and I realized suddenly that I had not thought of either of them since entering the old man's squalid little hut. I felt rotten, and my prospects were not especially pleasing, but I was moving again, and that made a world of difference. It was the sitting still that had driven me half mad, that and the damned rain. Now at least I had something to do, a particular direction in which to point myself. I had to work for the French liberation of Indochina, that it might take its rightful place alongside Quebec and Algeria and Madagascar.

*   *   *

'You have changed,' the old man said. 'Your whole face, it is very much different. You no longer look like a Frenchman.'

I never had, but that was beside the point. I put on the clothing he had brought me, a pair of loose-fitting olive drab trousers, a tan tunic, a pair of more elaborate sandals than I had been wearing. A large white coolie-style hat completed my costume and covered my shaggy brown hair, which had not been a part of the image I had wanted to project. I would have preferred to dye my hair black but couldn't think of a way to manage that. Shoe polish would have done the trick, but where does one come upon shoe polish in the wilds of Laos?

Outside, a hump-backed bullock stood hitched to a rickety cart. The cart was piled high with straw. If I rescued Tuppence, I thought, she could hide under the straw while I drove the cart. If I found Dhang instead, I could hide under the straw while he drove the cart. If I didn't rescue anyone, I could hole up somewhere and cook the bullock over a straw fire. If I was captured, the bullock could work for the greater glory of the beautiful France. If . . .

I was still a little feverish. It would come and go, waves of dizziness and nausea. I wondered if I could possibly have contracted rabies. Maybe I should have let the ghoulish doctor put needles in my brain. At least, I thought, I couldn't have plague. Or cholera. What did that leave? Jungle rot, malaria, typhus, typhoid fever, dengue fever, trench mouth, gonorrhea—I could have almost anything, I decided.

'Are you all right?'

'I'm fine,' I said. 'A slight touch of *la grippe*. I guess I'd better go now.'

'I have brought food—'

'I had some rice. I don't think I'd better eat anything more just now.' My stomach toyed with the notion of returning what I had already eaten, but I managed to change its mind for it. 'I wonder if you have heard any news of five black persons who were brought this way. Perhaps they are now in Tao Dan.'

'Five black persons.'

'Four men and a woman.'

'I have little contact with the world here. I sit in my hut, I work in the fields—'

'They might have passed this way any time within the last few weeks. They came from Thailand.'

'I know there are prisoners in Tao Dan. I have heard talk, but no one mentioned their color.'

'Perhaps it is they.'

'Perhaps. Are they the reason for your presence in this accursed land?'

'In a way.'

'You must be very cautious in Tao Dan. The times are dangerous, and the military police act with abandon. You speak the Khmer tongue, but when you came to the door of my hut, I knew at once that your accent was not of these parts. You would do well to speak as little as possible.'

'I know.'

'There are many among us who speak French, but of course it would not do for you to do so. It would be a hazard.'

'I'll try to keep silent as much as I can.'

'That is good.' He smiled shyly. 'I have brought a flask of rice wine that we might drink together. It is a poor local product. In the old days we would drink cognac, would we not? This is an inadequate substitute, but you would do me a great honor to drink with me.'

We drank a pasty white rice wine from a round tin flask. We drank to the glory of France, to Charles de Gaulle, to Napoleon, to Louis Quatorze. He capped the flask and told me to take it along with me, and somehow I managed not to. Somehow, too, I managed not to vomit up the pasty white rice wine. God knows how.

*   *   *

The fastest way to travel by bullock cart involves walking in front and tugging the bullock by a rope. This method is only slightly slower than walking alone unencumbered by bullock or cart, and considerably faster than riding in the cart and letting the bullock set the pace. I tried walking for a while but gave it up when I felt myself beginning to perspire. I didn't want to sweat the tobacco juice off of my face, so I got into the creaking cart and let the bullock have it with a bamboo switch. This didn't exactly put him in the thoroughbred league, but that was probably just as well; given the condition of the road—bumpy—and the condition of the cart—dilapidated—I don't think a fast trip would have been advisable. I sat on the pile of straw, hunched forward to keep as much of my face hidden as possible, and let the bullock proceed at his own pace toward Tao Dan.

I spent the ride getting into character, teaching my eyes and my lips to behave as I wanted them to, teaching my body to adapt itself to the stance of a Laotian peasant. As my bullock and I neared the town, we passed other carts and an occasional car heading in the opposite direction. Now and then someone called a greeting, to which I would nod and mumble. Hardly an acid test, but I was encouraged by the fact that I did not seem to be attracting any attention.

Tao Dan turned out to be a rather busy little town, the marketplace and seat of government for the surrounding countryside. Ramshackle round huts with peaked roofs alternated with squat buildings of white-washed concrete block. The streets were very narrow and extremely crowded. I was a new hand at the subtleties of guiding a bullock through heavy pedestrian traffic and after my beast came very close to trodding upon a little yellow infant, I gave up riding him and walked in front of him, my hat down over as much of my forehead as possible and my head and shoulders stooped. I made my way through a market street where old women sat selling bunches of indefinable vegetables, turned a corner, made my way through the local cattle market, shrugged off a variety of offers for my bullock, and generally drifted through the busy little town. It would have helped if I had known precisely who or what I was looking for, but I didn't. It would also have helped if I had felt better physically. I was perspiring again and was sure it would have an undesirable effect upon my complexion. I had the feeling that my digestive system might be ruined beyond repair, and my head was beginning to throb, a persistent ache that began at the base of my skull and worked its way forward from there.

What had become of Dhang?

I decided that he must have found the object of his search, but it seemed unlikely that he could still be busy with a woman. Even taking his youth and the fervor of his desire into consideration, the fact remained that one could only continue that particular activity for a certain amount of time. Of course, I thought, if he had given full vent to his desires, he might well have driven himself past the point of exhaustion. Even so, a night's sleep would have brought him awake again. Of course he might have resumed the original activity, but I hated to think it of him. We were friends, after all, and I couldn't believe he would leave me shivering in the underbrush forever while he screwed himself silly.

What, for that matter, had become of Tuppence and the Kendall Bayard Quartet? I had the feeling that they were the prisoners of whom the old man had spoken and that they were somewhere in Tao Dan. But where were political prisoners lodged in Tao Dan? I didn't know and I didn't trust myself to ask directions.

I found one street that was a little less crowded than the others and hitched the bullock at the curb, tying his lead rope to a small concrete pillar erected for that express purpose. I shuffled along the street, then followed a small crowd of men into what seemed to be a cafe. Inside, men were drinking out of small handleless cups of tea. I couldn't have any tea because I didn't have any money. I moved to the rear of the cafe and tried to stay as deep in the shadows as possible. A dozen conversations went on at once around me. I listened to them in turn. The dialect was difficult for me to follow, and most of the conversations seemed to revolve upon the various problems inherent in the life of a peasant in Laos. The agricultural trade terms were largely unfamiliar ones, and I was pretty much at sea.

Until at length I heard a large, heavy man with a deep voice begin to talk about a criminal event that had transpired during the night. A small crowd gathered around him, anxious for details. I shouldered my way

130

forward and listened to the storyteller.

He knew his trade well, beginning slowly, letting the excitement build. 'And so you know the girl of whom I speak,' he said. 'Her father is the commanding officer of the troop garrison. Just a young thing, she is, with the softest and purest skin, and a waist one could span with one's hands, and breasts exquisitely shaped like cups of tea, and hair like fine black silk . . .'

He paused for a chorus of oohs and ahhs.

'And this stranger appeared, no one knows from where. A young man, crude in his ways, and followed the girl down the street. Some say she did not know she was being followed'—he lowered his voice—'and others say she well knew a man was behind her, and let her hips sway from side to side, eh? Eh?'

A low giggle rose up from the crowd.

'And he followed her, or perhaps she led him, into the house of her father. The house of her father!' The crowd bubbled at the thought, a mixture of indignation from the puritans and grudging respect from the libertines. 'And in the house of her father, in the bed of her father, this wayward one prepared to take her. Some say he meant to force himself upon her and to overcome her resistance with beatings and terror'—again the voice went conspiratorially soft—'and others have it that no terror was necessary, that the girl would have willingly participated in what he wished!'

More hubbub from his listeners. It may not astonish you to learn that I had guessed the identity of the male participant in the drama. Poor Dhang, I thought. I hoped at least that he had attained the object of his desires before they killed him. At least he would have died happy.

But such was not the case.

'Fortunately,' the fat man continued, 'the chastity of the little one was preserved. Fortunately her own father arrived in the nick of time, reaching his beloved daughter's side before the culprit could complete his evil mission. With tears of frustration in his beady eyes the criminal was led away screaming.'

I could well believe it.

'And the criminal?' someone demanded.

'He shall receive the punishment that is his due.'

'Death?'

'What else?'

What else indeed? Dhang, I thought wearily, led a profoundly uncharmed life. First he had attempted to ravish a girl during the Week of Tears and Sighs, and the tears and sighs were all his own. And now, when he had settled on a succulent young Laotian girl, he had had the ill luck to select the daughter of the most powerful man in Tao Dan, the commander of the military garrison. It did not surprise me that he had been sentenced to death. But had the sentence been carried out yet?

Someone else asked the same question. 'He shall die this evening,' the storyteller replied. 'By nightfall'—he pointed off to his left—'his head shall decorate a post at the command headquarters.'

Not, I thought, if I could help it. Poor Dhang! I thought of the times during the night when I had accused him of treachery while he had trembled under the sentence of death. No doubt he had had the opportunity to betray me then. He could have attempted to tell them my whereabouts in exchange for his freedom. But he had kept his silence, and now, somehow, I had to find a way to free him.

I slipped unquestioned from the cafe. I stood for a moment on the sidewalk, getting my bearings. Then I retrieved my bullock and led him off in the direction the storyteller had indicated. The streets of Tao Dan were a maze, and I had to stop to ask directions to the command headquarters. I managed to select a myopic old gentleman who didn't seem to pay much attention to my non-Laotian face.

He pointed the way and mumbled directions. I walked on, hauling the bullock along behind me. I turned a corner as indicated and stopped in front of a large whitewashed concrete building from which an unfamiliar flag was flying.

There was no question about it—this was the place. The armed guards at attention on either side of the front doors indicated this, but something else confirmed it beyond question. There was a row of high metal posts off to the side of the doorway, one of which the storyteller had said Dhang's head would decorate.

Four posts were already decorated. I stood, holding the bullock's rope with one hand and my own jaw with the other, and gazed horrified at the four disembodied black heads of the Kendall Bayard Quartet.

CHAPTER TEN

Bad as it is to discover a worm in an apple, it is considerably more unpleasant to find half a worm in an apple. By the same token, there is something infinitely more grisly in the discovery of a portion of a corpse than in stumbling upon the deceased as a unit. I stared at the heads of the four musicians, and they stared back at me. I blinked, but they did not go away. They went on staring.

'American devil dogs,' said a voice at my elbow. 'Thieves and conspirators captured by our noble soldiers. See how their sightless eyes shine with evil.'

I swayed on my feet. A hand gripped my arm. I turned shakily and looked down into a gnarled and wrinkled face. 'You are so pale, young one,' the old woman said. 'Have you an illness?'

'I do not feel well.'

She looked over my shoulder at the four black heads. 'The spectacle bothers you?'

'I have never before seen such a sight.'

'Nor have I. For all time I had thought that the American devils were white, like the accursed French. But now it seems that they are black devils. You have the pallor of a white devil yourself, young one. You are not of Tao Dan.'

'I have come from the north.'

'Ah, there is a northern touch to your speech! I thought I had recognized it. What is your village?'

My mind whirled. 'I am from the countryside,' I said helplessly.

'Which village lies nearest to your home?'

'Kao Pectate,' I said. The diseased spirit offers up its own unbidden puns. I said Kao Pectate because, at the moment, I damned well needed it, but when I realized what I'd said, I wanted to crawl under a flat rock. The old crone was still clinging to my arm like a barnacle to a ship—a foundering ship, in this instance.

'I have never heard of this town,' she said.

'It is many days travel from Tao Dan.'

'So it may be.'

I felt it might be time to change the subject. 'They have told me that another devil is to be

135

beheaded,' I said.

'A madman. He attacked a young girl last evening.'

'I was told that there was a woman. A black woman.'

The hag peered shrewdly at me. 'Some say that this is so. Others say that it is not. There is little talk in Tao Dan of the black woman, and few have heard of her. Who told you she was within the command headquarters?'

'There was talk in another village.'

'Oh?'

I felt increasingly horrible. I didn't want to look at the old woman, who was behaving more and more like an agent for the Pathet Lao's secret police, and my only alternative was to watch the four heads baking in the morning sun.

'The sex criminal,' I said desperately. 'When is he to be killed?'

'Today.'

'At what hour?'

'It is of no importance, young one. All executions are carried out within the building. Then the head is brought outside for display.' She clucked her tongue in disappointment. 'In old times criminals and devils were put to death in the public square, where all could see. And it was not done with a single stroke of the sword, either. All executions began at noon, with the sun high in the sky, and often the condemned man would not draw his last gulp

136

of air until the sun had set.' She sighed, remembering. 'And the entire populace would come to view the spectacle, and the peasants from miles around would make their way into Tao Dan. Much business was done on such days. The cafes carried on a great trade. It is with sadness that I witness the disappearance of the ancient customs.'

'But this criminal—when will he die?'

She eyed me suspiciously. 'Why does it concern you? Are you of the same blood as this crazed one?'

'A wager. A man at a cafe, we wagered on the time of death.'

She nodded, at ease now. This made perfect sense to her; the Laos, like the Thais, will gamble on almost anything. Like the Siamese, they raise specimens of *Betta splendens*, hazarding great sums on the outcome when two male fish attempt to assert their respective territorial rights in a small bowl. That two strangers should bet on the time of a third stranger's death was wholly reasonable.

'Then, you must wait for the officials to determine the outcome of your wager,' she said. 'The criminal will die by evening prayers, but the exact time I do not know.'

*   *   *

I managed to get away from her. I took my bullock's lead rope in hand and headed him around the corner. A few blocks from the command headquarters I picked out another hitching post and tethered the bullock. I was sweating freely now and had to sit down somewhere before I collapsed. I climbed on top of the mound of straw in the cart, stretched out, and put my hat over my face. I had seen natives resting in this fashion and hoped I would look ordinary enough.

My mind simply wasn't functioning. The stark horror of those four heads atop those poles had evidently had dire effects upon a brain already numbed by a progressively heightening fever. I tried to put myself into the Yogic relaxation state, tensing and relaxing muscle groups in turn, letting myself go utterly limp, blanking my mind. To do this properly takes twenty minutes, which I couldn't afford, and a healthy mind and body, which I couldn't supply. I gave myself a few minutes to loosen up and unwind a bit, and then I tried putting together what I knew.

The Kendall Bayard Quartet was beyond salvation, at least in this world. For reasons that remained unfathomable to me, some in power had seen fit to separate their heads from their bodies, displaying their heads publicly and doing God-knew-what with the rest of them.

Tuppence was probably inside the building, but maybe she wasn't. She was probably going to be executed, but that was no foregone conclusion, and official policy seemed to be to pretend she had never existed in the first place. That seemed like a sensible policy, I thought idly; if I had followed it, I would have stayed in New York.

Dhang was definitely inside the building, where he would remain until they put him to death for rape. Attempted rape, actually—the poor son of a bitch was going to die without getting the only thing on earth he really wanted. Sometime within the next several hours he would be executed.

I wondered what part of him they would hang on the post. If the punishment were to fit the crime . . .

I decided I didn't want to think about it.

There were more important things to think about. I had to find a way to get into the command post, had to locate and free Tuppence and Dhang, and then had to get out again. Then I would have to find a way to get out of Laos or at least into the comparative safety of the southern part of the country, but all of that was a bridge that could be crossed when it was reached, not before.

Step One—get in. Step Two—rescue Tuppence and Dhang. Step three—get out.

Fine.

But Step One stumped me all by itself. Get in? How? Get the bullock to kick a hole in the side of the building, I thought wildly. Throw a stone at a cop and get arrested. Or rape somebody—that way I'd be sure of winding up in the sex offenders' cell with Dhang. Slug somebody, steal a uniform, and march importantly past the guards and through the corridors. Create a diversion—set fire to half the city, and when the guards ran to see what was happening, make a beeline for Tuppence and Dhang.

I sighed. Everything seemed quite hopeless. My assets were limited: a bullock, a cart, some straw, the clothes I was wearing, and, if I wanted to go back for them, a mud-clogged rifle and a machine pistol, and a flashlight that was missing a battery. I also had one ally: a broken-down old Francophile.

If Dhang hadn't managed to get himself caught, there might have been a chance. There would have been two of us instead of one, and one to rescue instead of two, which would make an immediate change in the odds. Still more important, the time element might not be so crucial. We could have taken our time and made our plans, and Dhang himself could have passed easily in the crowds, and the two of us working together might have come up with a way to get Tuppence out of there.

But I didn't have Dhang's help now. And by getting caught he had put a tight time limit on the game. If I was going to rescue him, I had to bring it off before evening prayers, whenever precisely that was. Because by then he'd have his head on a post.

A chill caught me up, and I fought it, bringing my knees up to my stomach and wrapping my arms around them. I was getting fever cramps in my arms and legs, and my head felt like the before half of an aspirin commercial. James Bond never got sick, I thought resentfully. James Bond never had to worry about washing or shaving or changing his clothes, or finding a toilet when amoebas played jump-rope with his lower intestine. James Bond, in my particular situation, would pluck a button off his cuff and flick it at command headquarters, whereupon all of the enemy would be blown to bits to the tune of 'Rule, Britannia.'

James Bond was a hell of a lot better suited to this sort of idiocy than I was.

*   *   *

The old man drew on his pipe. Moisture gurgled in the pipestem. He took it from his mouth and looked in turn at it and at me. In his heavily accented French he said, 'My young friend, I do not know how I can help you.'

Neither did I. I had left Tao Dan to lead my bullock all the way back to the old man's hut, not because I thought he would really be able to help me but because I couldn't think of anything else to do. He took one look at me and made me lie down on his straw mattress and cover myself with his few blankets. While I

141

babbled wildly about Tuppence and Dhang he poured cup after cup of strong herb tea into me. It came out through my pores in rivers of sweat. My stomach calmed down after a while, and finally the fever broke.

'You must sleep,' he assured me. 'You must spend a week doing nothing but sleeping and drinking the tea. Or you will die.'

And then I had told him why I couldn't sleep, not the medical reasons but the immediate, practical ones. A Senegalese princess and a Thai agent of France were under sentence of death in Tao Dan. It was my mission to rescue them and rush them to safety in Paris. In their hands, I said, they held the future of the French colonial empire in the Orient.

Perhaps, I suggested, he had comrades in the area, other men who had known the glory of French leadership, other men whose thoughts and feelings were akin to his own. Men who would help us in our noble task, men who would join with us to . . .

As rhetoric goes, it certainly went. I don't think I could do it justice in English, but the French language is an ideal vehicle for the expression of such sentiments. The speech fired the old man's blood—it was even beginning to rouse me, for that matter—but at the end he merely shook his head.

'I am such a man,' he said unhappily, 'but I know no others. This is a nation of slaves and

142

fools and traitors, and the times are bad. Here there are only knaves who bow down to those in power and peasants whose thoughts never rise beyond their rice bowls and their yokes and plows. If the Communists seize a man's bullock, he puts the yoke upon his wife's shoulders. If they beat him, he apologizes. If they kick him, he polishes their shoes with his tongue.'

'If we had just a few men—'

'But there are none but myself.'

I sank back on the straw pallet. I had succeeded only in wasting more precious time, the time I had spent walking from the village and the time it would take me to return to it. It was hopeless, and I should have known as much, but there was nothing else to be done and no one else to whom I could turn.

'You say that this son and daughter of the beautiful France are in the command headquarters?'

I gulped herb tea. Hopeless, I thought. Better to stay on the old man's floor until the fever either ran its course or killed me. Better to keep out of Tao Dan entirely and later to make my way back through Thailand to Bangkok. Better to let them lop off Dhang's head and Tuppence's head. *If you can keep your head when all about you are losing theirs and blaming it on you—*

'My young friend, are you awake?'

'Yes, why?'

'You did not seem to hear me. I asked if your allies are being held in the command headquarters.' I nodded. 'And there is how much time until the murder?'

'A few hours.'

'If you could gain access to the command post, if you could manage to slip inside, would you have any chance of success?'

'Possibly, I don't know. But the guards—'

'Perhaps I can dispose of the guards.'

'How?'

He held up a hand and waved the question aside. An odd smile played on his thin old lips. I finished the tea, and he dipped my cup into the pot and filled it again. I sipped it and looked up at him. He was humming the 'Marseillaise.'

'*Le jour de gloire*,' he sang softly. His eyes flashed at me. 'Perhaps the day of glory has indeed arrived, my little friend. Perhaps it is so. Do you think it is possible?'

'I don't understand.'

'We must return to town,' he said. 'Finish your tea, there is time. I will lead the animal, and you must ride in the cart. You will need your strength later in the day. The day of glory. When you leave the building, how will you flee the town? Have you a plan?'

'No.'

'There is a river east of the town. If you had a small boat moored at the bank, it would be a great asset to you, would it not? Gold will buy a boat. There is enough left of what you have given me.'

'But—'

'No time, not now. Finish your tea, that is a good boy. Can you get to your feet? I will help you—'

'I can manage.'

'Good, very good. And now we will go to town, but first you must darken your face once more. Was it my tobacco that you used?'

'Yes.'

'I hope there is enough left to do the job. Go ahead, it is all right. I will not need more now. Go ahead.'

The taste of the tobacco almost made me sick again, but I chewed it and rubbed the resulting liquid into my face. I gave my hands and forearms the same treatment. It didn't take so long this time, perhaps because the fever was beginning to endow me with a yellowish color all my own.

'And now we go,' he said. 'You will mingle with the crowds, you will stay close to the entrance of the command headquarters. I will see to the rest.'

'What time—'

'You will know when it is time, my friend I only hope that it can be done before it is too late.'

CHAPTER ELEVEN

I don't remember very much of the ride to town. I kept telling myself over and over again that I couldn't have plague or cholera and that I had not yet been bitten by a rabid skunk. Nor had I walked through any caves cluttered with bat crap. I would tell myself this, and then the fever would pick up steam again, and I would become slightly delirious. I was in fairly good control of myself, however. Each time I had to vomit, I managed to lean over the side of the cart.

In Tao Dan the old man parked the bullock and took me to a little restaurant. He knew the proprietor and spoke rapidly to him before leading me to a small booth at the rear. Then he pressed a few well-creased little bank notes into my hand.

'I have told him to continue bringing you cups of herbal tea,' he said. 'I have said that you have a weakness of the brain and cannot speak clearly. Thus it will not be necessary for you to say anything, and you may remain here until I return. No one will disturb you.'

I nodded.

'I will be back shortly. I will arrange for a boat. I had thought to take you with me, but it may be more readily done this way. Then I will tell you how to find the boat after I return.

You will wait here? You will not move?'

'There is little time—'

'I know. I shall not be long.'

He left. I looked down at the table top. It was wooden, and the finish had long ago been worn away. My eyes saw intricate patterns in the scarred surface, patterns alive with aesthetic implications. Fever does weird things to one's mind.

Then the waitress was bringing my cup of herb tea. She was a tiny thing and looked to be about twelve years old. I thought at first that she was a very pretty child, but when I looked more closely, I saw that one of her eyes was missing. The empty socket was black inside. She smiled shyly and set the tea down before me. I tried not to look at her face. I felt tears welling up behind my own eyes and blamed them on the fever. The world, after all, is filled with blind children who envy the one-eyed ones, and legless men who envy cripples, and millionaires who envy billionaires. One has to maintain a sense of proportion . . .

I smiled at the girl. I held my thumb and forefinger an inch apart, brought them to my lips, and made chewing motions.

'You are to have only tea,' she said. 'You are not to have food. The man said.'

I shook my head, smiled again, and went through the routine once more. This time I made motions of chewing and spitting, chewing and spitting.

'Not food?'

I shook my head.

She smiled, pleased with the game. 'Show me again.' I did. 'Betel nut? You wish betel nut?'

I smiled and nodded enthusiastically. 'I will get it for you. I ask my father if you may have. You wait.'

She rushed away. In a few moments she came tripping back with a slice of betel nut wrapped in the usual leaf. The flavoring agent was different from that used in Dhang's betel but by no means unpleasant. I smiled my thanks, chewed, spat. The girl giggled happily, made a small but very courtly bow, and scampered away.

I found myself thinking of Minna and hoping that she was all right. I knew that Kitty Bazerian would take good care of her, and I was privately convinced that the child was sufficiently adaptable to get along almost anywhere; she possessed both charm and pragmatism far beyond her years. But she was happiest at home with me in the apartment on 107th Street, which was why I would undoubtedly never get around to having her adopted, or sending her to school, or doing any of the things one really ought to do with a child her age.

Thoughts of Minna drew me out of my role, and I caught myself letting my eyes widen and my mouth relax. I narrowed my eyes to slits once more and pursed my lips. I had to get out of this mess, I told myself. After all, I wasn't entirely a carefree adventurer any more. I was a man with responsibilities—Minna, Todor, another child on the way. I had to get a grip on myself.

Perhaps the betel nut was an imperfect idea. I had ordered it because I wanted it, which seemed motivation enough at the time. But the slight narcotic properties of the betel nut seemed to be working in tandem with the fever. My head was doing unusual things. From time to time I would catch myself staring off into space with the purposeless intensity of the catatonic, spending endless minutes in stoic contemplation of nothing whatsoever, with not a thought passing through my mind. Then I would force myself to move an arm or a foot, to drink some of the ever-present tea, to chew and spit.

When my teacup was empty, the girl returned for it and brought it back full again. I handed her all of the notes the old man had left with me; I didn't want to run up a tab higher than my bankroll. She started to give some of them back to me, and I motioned her to keep the lot. She smiled, and her eye brightened. She returned again in a little while and slipped me a handful of betel, giggling as she did so and either winking or blinking, whatever you prefer. I put the betel in the pocket of my tunic.

My time sense was completely shot. When the old man sat down opposite me—I hadn't even noticed his approach, which shows how magnificently I was functioning—I had no idea whether he had been gone an unusually short time or an exceedingly long time. I really did not know. It could have been fifteen minutes or several hours.

In French he whispered, 'It is arranged. I have purchased a boat. It is small, but I believe it will accommodate three persons. You and the Thai and the Princess.'

'What about yourself?'

'Do not worry yourself about me. Now'—his finger traced lines on the scarred table top— 'we are here. Here is the command headquarters. You see? The front of the building here, a rear entrance here. Down this way is a street that leads to the river. It runs just so. You follow me? You take that street and do not leave it, and it will lead you directly to the bank of the river. The boat is hidden in the rushes perhaps fifty paces in this direction. You see the route you must take? This way from the building, and down the road to its end, and then to your left and along the shore perhaps fifty paces, perhaps sixty. The boat is well hidden, I cut reeds and placed them atop it. You will be able to find it?'

'I think so.'

'I am sure that you will. There will be very little time. You must hurry into the building

150

and liberate the two prisoners and hurry out again as quickly as possible. You may find this useful.'

He put a hand under the table, and I reached to take what he handed me. It was a dagger with an eight-inch blade, razor sharp, with deep blood grooves running the length of the blade on either side. The hilt was covered with tightly wrapped leather. The dagger had not been washed since its last use, and there were traces of blood in the grooves. I concealed it as well as I could in a fold of the tunic.

'Go, now,' the old man said. 'We are in time, your friends have not yet been executed. Get as close to the entranceway as you can. When the moment is at hand, seize it. Do not spend time watching me.'

'What are you going to do?'

He looked at me, and over my shoulder, and miles past me. Perhaps he was seeing a parade in the Place de la Concorde.

'I shall do what I must,' he said.

'But—'

'It is time.' A smile. 'The day of glory has arrived. Do not ask questions, young friend. Go now. The day of glory has arrived.'

I put both hands on the table top and pushed myself to my feet. The day of glory has arrived, I told myself. My knees buckled. I took a deep breath and walked unsteadily to the doorway. My little waitress blinked good-bye. I stepped out into the heat of the glaring afternoon sun, waited for a moment to get my bearings, then found my way quickly to the command headquarters.

The four heads stared at me as before, but this time they had no effect upon me. Perhaps I was prepared; perhaps the fever and the betel nut had combined to render me impervious to horror. I looked at the heads, and they looked back, and I walked past them to the side of the entranceway, where notices were posted on a bulletin board. Some were hand-lettered, others were printed, and all of them were equally meaningless to me. I can speak Khmer but cannot read it at all and after I had looked at a few notices, I found it hard to believe that anybody could read it. It has frequently occurred to me that the high illiteracy rate in certain countries is at least partially attributable to the impenetrability of their alphabets. It amazes me that people learn to speak at all, let alone read and write. I went on scanning the bulletin board. The fever caught me, then let me go. For a moment I was quite unsteady and didn't think I could stay on my feet, and I moved to one side and turned around, leaning against the building in what I hoped was a casual fashion. The street was beginning to fill with the local citizenry, all of whom seemed interested in the command post. Though public executions had been abolished, it was evidently quite the thing to watch new heads being installed on the ceremonial head posts. Perfectly reasonable, I decided. With no movie theater and no television, the people needed something to take their minds off their troubles.

I slipped my hand under my tunic and touched the handle of the dagger. Its presence was somehow reassuring. I looked at the squat concrete building. If we left it by its rear door, we would have to run off to the right to the street the old man had indicated, then turn to the left and follow that street to the river, then look off to the left some fifty paces for the boat. I pictured his finger tracing the route on the table top and I closed my eyes and fixed the image of his map in my mind.

In the street a jeep made its way through the crowd. The driver confirmed the popular notion of the Oriental view that human life is cheap, driving with a fine disdain for the throngs in front of him. Magically the crowd melted aside just in time to let him pull to a stop in front of the building. The driver remained in the car. Two men climbed out of the back seat. One of them was middle-aged and looked important. The other younger and in a less impressive uniform, hurried to open the door for him. The guards stood aside, and the two men walked on into command headquarters.

Wonderful, I thought. By the time I made my move, half the soldiers in Laos would be inside the concrete structure. I looked around, wondering what the old man had planned. For a moment I had thought he might have organized some sort of riot, with the mob storming the building, but the crowd did not have the look of potential rioters. They were just a mass of bored yokels waiting for something to happen.

I chewed a fresh piece of betel and spat a stream of red juice at the dusty ground. The sun burned down. The deluge of the night before was barely a memory, and what had been mud a few hours ago was now baked as hard as earthenware. I chewed and spat and, like the mindless crowd, I waited for something to happen.

Then something happened.

I didn't even recognize the old man at first, but I stared at him anyhow, just like everyone else. He was a sight. He was riding in my cart, and my bullock was pulling it, and all of that was normal enough, but that was where normalcy stopped. For the bullock was moving faster than it had ever moved in its life, faster, I suspect, than any bullock had ever moved since the species first evolved. The bullock tore through the crowd like a bull at Pamplona, tossing its head and snorting, bouncing the little cart on the bumpy roadway, while the old man prodded its rump with fire.

I do not speak metaphorically. The old colonial boy held a long stick like a shepherd's crook, and on the end of that stick was a rag soaked in kerosene or something of the sort, and the rag was burning. He kept poking the flaming end of the stick into the tormented end of the bullock, and the results were spectacular.

All hell broke loose. The crowd stampeded. The jeep parked in front happened to be in the way, and the bullock came down on its hood and struck a mighty blow against the forces of automation. The animal caromed off the wrecked vehicle, tossed its head wildly, then charged for a mass of onlookers. They broke and ran; some of them got away and some of them did not.

The guards didn't know what to do. They had drawn their guns and were now waving them uncertainly in the air, evidently feeling that the situation could be solved only by a show of force but not knowing where the force ought to be directed. And through it all the old man prepared for his finest hour. *The day of glory has arrived—*

He was in costume, for one thing. He wore the uniform of a French Legionaire. God knows where he found it; perhaps he had kept it hidden as a relic of better times. It fit him like a glove on a pencil. The pants covered his feet and the jacket's sleeves came down well over his hands, and the shriveled little old man inside disappeared completely. He paused, kept the fire away from the bullock's rear for a moment, and his little voice rang out over the crowd.

'Long live King Charles de Gaulle! Long live the beautiful France! Lafayette is here! Long live Napoleon! To hell with Marx! To hell with Lenin! To hell with the Pathet Lao! To hell with Mao Tse-tung! Long live Jeanne d'Arc!'

Everyone's attention was drawn to him. The doors to the command post were open, and soldiers from within crowded the doorway, staring out at the wild old man with the wild young bullock. I could have pushed through them without their paying the slightest bit of attention to me, but at the moment I was utterly transfixed by his display. Wild bullocks couldn't have moved me.

' "Allons, enfants de la patrie—" '

Singing the 'Marseillaise' at the top of his lungs, he began waving a tin can around madly. He splashed something from it, soaking the straw around him, soaking the fine French Legion uniform, soaking the flanks of the unfortunate bullock.

Then, still singing bravely, he brought the day of glory to its peak. He touched his torch to the straw beneath his feet. And, as the straw and the cart and the bullock and the old man burst suddenly into flame, with the maddened bullock veering sharply to his right and crashing head-on into a cluster of ramshackle wooden huts, with bullets flying overhead, and

156

with the final death-echoes of the French national anthem sounding around me, I drew my dagger and rushed into the building.

CHAPTER TWELVE

Behind me the crowd hooted and wailed hysterically. Soldiers rushed into the mob to stare mutely at the spreading fire. Someone began shooting at something. I moved quickly, mind and body oddly disassociated. At the head of the stairs a soldier blocked my path and snapped a command at me. I thrust the dagger hilt-deep into his chest. He gasped and died, and no one noticed. I drew the dagger free and entered the building.

The corridors inside were uniformly olive drab, floors and walls and ceilings, a study in institutional monotony. The entire place was in an uproar, with uniformed men barking commands and rushing to and fro. I too rushed to and fro, and to as little purpose. I felt like a moth who against all odds had managed to penetrate a screen and fly into a fireplace. I was a great success, but at any moment the flames would realize I was there and fry me to a crisp.

'Outside!' I bellowed. 'All men to their posts in the streets. At once!'

That got rid of a few of them, but there

were still too many soldiers around. I looked into one room, then another, but there was no sign of either Dhang or Tuppence. And I couldn't peek into every damned room in the place. There simply wasn't time; in a few moments the shock value of the old man's act would wear off, and somebody would begin to wonder just who in hell I was.

I started into a third room. A soldier on his way out met me with pistol in hand. If I had had time to think about it I would probably have stood there like a ninny while he shot me, but I acted without thought, plunging the dagger into his belly and ripping upward. He pitched forward, and I spun away from him and on down the corridor.

And promptly walked into another man. We bounced off one another, and I said 'Pardon me,' and he said 'Who are you?' and I looked at him, and he looked at me. His chest was full of medals and ribbons. He was the important-looking middle-aged man who had recently dismounted from the jeep in front.

He said, 'Seize this man!'

But I seized him first. I grabbed him by the shoulder and gave a yank, and he spun like a top and sagged against me. The top of his head came to just below my chin. I wrapped one arm around his chest and with the other hand I held the tip of the dagger to his throat.

'I just hope to God you're important,' I told him in English, 'or we're both going to wind up dead.'

He was saying something that I couldn't understand, which I guess made us even. A semicircle of armed men stood around us, their guns pointed at me. I worked my way backward so that my back was against a wall. I kept my grip on the important little man, and the tip of my dagger stayed within an inch of his throat.

'If you do not cooperate, you will die,' I told him, in Khmer this time. 'Tell your men to throw their weapons down upon the floor. Do this at once!'

He said something unintelligible. The soldiers were still holding their weapons.

'Tell them,' I said reasonably. I pricked the skin over his Adam's apple with the dagger. He was trembling in my grasp. His voice shaky, he conveyed my order to his men. Rifles and pistols bounced crazily on the bare concrete floor. One discharged, and a bullet ricocheted wildly from wall to ceiling to wall.

'The Thai who was taken prisoner last night,' I said. 'Where is he?'

'The ravisher of my daughter?'

So this was the commandant, I thought. 'That's the one,' I said. 'Where is he being held?'

'He is to die for his crimes.'

'He is to go free. Where is he?'

'What do you want with him?'

I prodded him again with the dagger. 'I shall

cut out your heart,' I said gently, 'and your liver, and I shall roast your intestines in the fire. Tell your men to lead us to the prisoner's cell. Do not waste time.'

'You will die.'

'Yes, but not right now. Give them the order.'

He barked it out, his voice cracking before he reached the end of the sentence. The men—there were about a dozen of them—led the way to a small room at the end of a long corridor to the right. They were a disorganized bunch, those soldiers. Their training had made no provision for such an emergency, and they did not know what they were supposed to do. They had been taught, like all good soldiers everywhere, to obey unquestioningly all orders of a superior officer and to avoid taking matters into their own hands. The little commander followed a still older code, the ancient law of self-preservation. And thus the men led the way to Dhang's cell, and the commander, pale and trembling, stared cross-eyed at the dagger that touched his throat.

More orders. A heavy iron door was unbolted and drawn open. At the far end of a dank, windowless room a half-naked Dhang, the upper portion of his body scarred badly with the marks of the lash, stood upon the tips of his toes. His hands were tied to a pipe overhead, and his toes just barely reached the ground. He did not seem to recognize me at first but stared ahead dully.

The sight of him infuriated me, and I came very close to ruining everything by killing the commandant then and there out of sheer pique. But I snapped out a brace of orders, which he conveyed to his men. They cut Dhang free, and he sprawled face-down on the floor. I shouted at him. He shook himself, looked up at me, then struggled to his feet.

'Heaven! You have come . . .'

I tossed him a chunk of betel. He popped it gratefully into his mouth. 'There's very little time,' I told Dhang. 'We have to get out of here.' I singled out one of the soldiers who was about Dhang's height and build and had the commandant tell him to get out of his uniform. He did this, and Dhang dressed himself in the soldier's clothing. He didn't exactly look as though he had been born to wear a uniform, but it wasn't a bad fit.

'I could have had her, Evan. So beautiful she was! And she wanted me, too. They said I tried to have her against her will, but in truth she wanted me. She—'

The commandant cursed and tried to make a lunge for Dhang. I tightened my grip on him.

'Such a sweet cunat,' Dhang went on. 'And in another moment she would have been mine, but then this pig had to intrude.' And he cleared his throat and spat in the commander's face.

I couldn't really blame him.

161

'No time now,' I said. 'We have to hurry. Tuppence is somewhere in the building. Have you seen her? The girl?'

'No.'

'We'll have to find her. Go back toward the front door and make sure it's locked. And pick up a couple of pistols from the floor, one for yourself and one for me.' I backed off toward the door, dragging the head man with me.

'Tell your men to sit down,' I ordered him. 'Tell them to seat themselves upon the floor and remain there until they are called.'

He did, and they did. We left the room with the dozen men inside it, and I toed the door shut, then bolted it. The fever hit suddenly, slamming me with a wave of dizziness and nausea. I swayed on my feet and very nearly dropped the dagger. I drew a deep breath and tried to catch hold of myself. The building, I thought, I had to get into the building. No, that was wrong, I was already inside the building, and now I had to find Tuppence and get out of it.

I spun the little man around and backed him against the wall. 'The girl,' I said. 'Where is she?'

'There is no girl.'

'The black girl.'

'There is no black girl.'

'Damn you, where is she?'

'There is no black girl.'

I transferred my dagger to my left hand,

made a fist of the right hand, and hit him in the mouth with it. He caromed off the wall and stumbled toward me. I hit him again. He sagged against the wall, wiping at the blood that trickled from his mouth.

'You may kill me if you wish,' he said stiffly. 'There is no black girl here. I will not tell you anything.'

I started to swing at him, then caught myself in time. Dhang was trotting down the hallway, moving gingerly over the floor. I found out later that they had beaten the soles of his feet. Dhang handed me a pistol and kept one for himself.

'There were soldiers there,' he told me.

'What happened?'

'They saw the uniform and thought I was one of them. I picked up the guns and shot them.' I hadn't even heard the shots. 'I closed the door, Heaven. But much is happening outside. Flames and screaming. We must get out of here.'

'This pig won't tell me where the girl is.'

'Shall I kill him?'

'No. We'll need him later.' I wished I could think straight. She had to be somewhere inside the building, I decided.

I cupped my hands and shouted. 'Tuppence! Tuppence, where are you? Tuppence!'

A muffled cry came in answer from off to the left. Dhang led the way, and I grabbed up the little commander, and we ran. I shouted,

163

and she called out in answer, and we kept running to the sound of her voice until we found the room.

The door was locked. The commander denied possession of a key, and there was no time to find out whether he was lying or not. I called out for Tuppence to stand aside, and put three bullets in the lock before it fell apart. The door flew open, and there was Tuppence.

'Evan, baby! Like where did you come from?'

'Later,' I said. 'This is Dhang, he's a friend, he doesn't speak English. This is the Lord High Everything-Else, he—'

'I know him,' she said contemptuously. She went on to describe him as a fulfiller of oedipal desires. 'How'd you get here, baby?'

'Later.'

'Kendall and Willie and Chick and Nile—'

'I know. Dead.'

'Goddamn.'

Dhang was chattering excitedly at my elbow. I didn't pay any attention to him. 'You can tell me about it later,' I told Tuppence. 'First we've got to get out of here. There's a boat waiting. We'll go out the back door and—'

'What's the matter, baby? You all right?'

I had stopped abruptly in mid-sentence. It was the fever, coming on worse than before. All of a sudden everything I looked at was tinted a furious red. I blinked the redness away and shook myself free of the fever's grip.

'I'm sick,' I said. 'I'll be all right once we get out of here. Follow me.' I gave the same order to Dhang, and I dragged the Lao commander along. Where was the back door? I had lost my bearings and wasn't sure.

But Tuppence said, 'Wait, cool it, Evan. We don't want to leave without the jewels.'

'The jewels?'

'The Siamese pretties. This mothering bastard has them locked up in his office. We can't leave them.'

'The hell with them. There's no time.'

'Won't take a minute.'

'I don't even know where his office is.'

'I do,' she said. 'I damn well should. His men dragged me to it once a day, regular as a clock.' She glared at the commander. 'You little bastard,' she said to him. To me she said, 'Once a day he had me brought to him. He has this mattress on the floor. He's full of class, this boy. Can't even afford a couch. Put me on the mattress, put himself on me, and wham and bam and not even a thank you, ma'am.' She hauled off and slapped him in the face, and his head bounced back.

'There's no time, Tuppence. Don't waste it talking.'

'Come on, then.'

I didn't care about the jewels. I didn't care about anything. I just wanted to get the hell out of there before I pitched over on my face. But it was easier to go along with her than to

165

argue about it. She led the way through a maze of corridors to another locked door. There was a pane of frosted glass in the door. It was the only door I had seen like that, evidently a special luxury, a great status symbol. I knocked out the glass with the butt of my pistol and reached through to unbolt the door.

There was a straw mattress on the floor, as Tuppence had said. She hurried past it without looking at it and tugged at a drawer of the desk. It wouldn't open.

The commander was making unhappy noises—he really didn't want us to get those jewels. Somehow this encouraged me. Anything that bothered him made me happy. I let Dhang cover him and went around the desk. I shot the lock off—guns have a multitude of uses—and Tuppence yanked open the drawer and hauled out two leather sacks.

'Wait till you get a look at these, Bwana. Your eyes shall roll in disbelief.'

'Later.'

'Like a king's ransom.'

'Or the ransom of a Senegalese princess.'

'Huh?'

'Later. Let's move.'

We moved. Tuppence took one sack of jewels, and Dhang carried the other. I twisted the commandant's arm behind his back in a hammerlock and propelled him in front of me, the muzzle of the pistol against the side of his neck. The fight had gone out of him now. With his men locked up, his prisoners liberated, and his jewels gone from his desk, he had lost all will to resist.

We located the back door. I hesitated in front of it, certain that we would open it to find ourselves surrounded by soldiers. There couldn't be too many of them, I decided. It seemed unlikely that too many men would be garrisoned at Tao Dan, and with several dead and a dozen locked inside Dhang's cell and more fighting the fires that the old man had started, I didn't expect too much of a welcoming committee. Dhang thrust the door open, and we went through it.

There was no one there. The noise from the other side of the building was deafening—shouts, screams, the staccato snapping of small arms fire. From the street we could see flames leaping everywhere. The fire was spreading throughout Tao Dan.

I tried to remember the old man's map. Off to the right, then to the left on the long street that ran to the river. Which was right and which was left? My head was mixing things up. I started in the wrong direction, then caught myself and turned around.

'Do we have to take this pig with us, Yevan?'

Dhang gestured at the commandant with his pistol.

'He will slow us down.'

'He could be a valuable hostage. If we run

into an armed patrol, his presence might save us.'

'Make him move faster.'

We hurried onward. The race to the river bank remains a blur in my mind. The fever seemed to be getting worse instead of better. Colors were unusually bright. My body took one path and my mind another, and I seemed to be racing along without paying any real attention to what I was doing. My head was overflowing with unexplained questions. Why had Tuppence and the quartet been kidnapped? Why were the men killed? Why was Tuppence kept alive? How did the jewels enter into it all? Who had stolen them, and for what purpose?

Somehow we found the right street and followed it to the river. I remember the whole thing very imperfectly, and the memory is mostly sensory—the heat of the road beneath my feet, burning through the thin soles of the sandals, the sun hot overhead, the furious pounding of my heart. There was no one behind us, but I was fairly certain that pursuit would come before very long, and so we ran, out of the village and past the stray huts on its outskirts, and onward to the bank of the river.

It was a broad river, the waters dark and muddy, the current swift, forming little whirlpools here and there. The bank was dense with undergrowth, reeds and bulrushes and sprawling vines and shrubs. We made our way along the river's edge and found the boat just where the old man had said it was. I would never have found it if I had not been looking for it. It was completely concealed among the reeds.

We removed the camouflage. Off in the distance small fishing boats sailed upon the river. I studied our craft. It was not the rowboat I had suspected but was more along the lines of the dugout canoes of the American Indians. A very large tree had been cut down and split in half, and a section of trunk some twelve feet long had been hollowed out, evidently by fire, with the charred center of the tree carefully removed until only a shell remained.

Tuppence studied the boat thoughtfully. 'We don't need him any more,' she said, pointing to the commandant. 'He's a good old hostage, but we have no use for him now.'

'We could take him.'

'Really, Evan.' She was swinging with her English accent now. 'There's scarcely room for three of us, and we have the jewels as well. We needn't waste space on a rapist and a murderer. He made me watch when he killed those four boys. He had their heads cut off. Rivers of blood.'

'So?'

'He's had a long life. I think it's time it ended.'

I still had the dagger. I handed it to her.

169

'Want to kill him yourself?' I asked. And she, of course, was supposed to do as the girls always do in the movies, clutching the dagger, studying it in horror, and then muttering something like *Oh, let him live with himself, that will be punishment enough for him* or *Oh, no, I couldn't, I couldn't* or *No, it's wrong, there must be an end to all of this wanton slaughter* or *If we kill him, then we are no better than he is* or any of those lines.

But Tuppence hadn't read the script. 'I'd bloody well love to,' she said, and fastened her small black hand around the butt of the dagger and advanced on the cowering commandant. He shrank from her; he seemed as much dismayed at a woman's being the instrument of his death as he did at dying in the first place. He let out a rather pathetic moan, and Tuppence sank the knife into his soft, round belly and ripped him wide open.

I threw up, but I think it was more the fever than the spectacle that caused it. The commandant made unpleasant noises for a time and then quietly died. Tuppence and Dhang helped me into the dugout. There was a single oar inside it, and we used it to push the boat free of the bank and out onto the waterway.

I sat in the stern, Dhang perched in the bow, and Tuppence was between us. Dhang had taken the oar and wanted to know in which direction we ought to proceed.

'Go with the current,' I said, pointing. 'We'll go that way whether we want to or not, so we might as well paddle in that direction.'

Tuppence wanted to know what we were saying, so I translated for her. Then Dhang asked what I was saying to the girl. I could see a potentially horrible situation developing, with myself in the middle of it. I told Tuppence in English that Dhang did not speak English and that I would relay to her whatever was important of my discussions with him but that we would all go crazy if I translated everything. Then I told Dhang approximately the same thing in Siamese, and then I leaned back in the dugout and watched birds diving for fish in the river and thought that perhaps Esperanto wasn't such a terrible idea after all.

I took a fresh piece of betel for myself and offered one to Dhang, but he said his slice had not yet lost its flavor. I popped the betel into my mouth. Tuppence wanted to know what the hell it was, and I told her.

'Man, you've really gone native,' she said.

'It's not bad once you get used to it.'

'Is that how come your teeth are black?'

'Yes.'

'Will you be able to get them clean later on?'

'I hope so.'

'What I could really use is a cigarette. I don't suppose you have one?'

'I don't smoke.'

171

'I'm hip, but you used to carry cigarettes for me.'

'This is a little different.'

'I know it, baby. I know a girl who's a betel nut. She's crazy for Ringo Starr. Sorry about that. I'll try it, what the hell.'

I gave her a piece of betel, and she chewed it and spat in the river. We were altogether a charming little group.

'You look terrible,' she said. 'Is that sunburn or from being sick?'

'A little of both,' I said. And I told her, too, about the cosmetic properties of tobacco juice. She thought that was very interesting but would be more interested personally in finding a way to reverse the process.

'What happens now, baby?'

'We just keep sailing. Later on we might be able to catch some fish for dinner, but meanwhile I think we should keep moving as fast as we can.'

'Uh-huh. Moving where?'

'Downstream.'

'Yeah, groovy. What I'm getting at is where does the stream go?'

'Oh,' I said.

'I said something wrong?'

'No,' I said. I shook my head groggily. I had somehow forgotten to ask the old man that little question. I had taken things step by step, and it seemed sufficient to get into the building and out of the building and locate the boat. I hadn't given too much thought to what would happen thereafter.

And I had no idea where the river was headed.

CHAPTER THIRTEEN

Birds wheeled high overhead, fish and water snakes swam alongside the dugout. The sun, overhead at first, was soon lost behind stands of tall timber and eventually set, presumably in the west. We seemed to be pointed in a general southerly direction, but the river made so many dips and turns that it was difficult to say with assurance. Before long it was difficult for me to say anything, with or without assurance. There was no herb tea aboard the little boat, and without it the fever grew worse instead of better. I huddled in the stern of the canoe while the world went on around me and I paid it as little attention as I possibly could.

'You must sleep,' said Dhang in Siamese. 'You must sleep,' said Tuppence in English. I agreed with both of them, but there was very little I could do about it. I kept my eyes closed most of the time because I couldn't see very well anyway, and the light intensified my headache. I thought for a time that I might sleep after all, that the fury of the disease might induce some sort of coma.

This didn't happen. What did happen was very odd, and I'm still not sure that I understand it. I gather that I descended into some sort of delirium. I wasn't raving, actually. I stayed quite still and remained generally silent. But I slipped in and out of an eerie waking dream during which periods of fantasy and reality overlapped, so that it was impossible to tell which was which, and even now I cannot be entirely certain what was real and what was imagined.

A variety of this, I suspect, is what alcoholics experience in delirium tremens. I have heard that one of the problems of the alcoholic is that he does not dream; he is so besotted with drink that he falls immediately into a comatose state too deep for dreaming. And dreams, the psychologists have discovered, are a necessary means of expunging various tensions and strains and doubts and fears. So the theory goes that the alcoholic in the DT's goes through a sort of waking dream, and the pink elephants he sees while conscious are just a version of the ogres that creep through the average person's nightmares.

I had understood the theory before. Now I found out what it was all about. It was not at all pleasant, and perhaps the best thing to be said for it is that most of it has since faded from memory. The parts that I recall now include things that probably did happen and things that certainly did not.

Fragments—

'It was a groovy trip until those cats came down on us, Evan. And Bangkok was like the best part of it. The group had this very tough sound, and I was in good voice and all. And the king was too much. You hear how all these celebrities are jazz fans, and it turns out that what they have is one old Bix Beiderbecke 78 stuck in a closet somewhere, but the king of Siam really digs. He truly does. He sat in on clarinet for a while. I thought he would be bloody awful, but his technique is good, and he knows where it's at. Chick went through some pretty deep chord patterns, and the king never did shake out. He stayed with it all the way to the end . . .

'I dug Bangkok, I truly did. They have this floating fruit market, I never saw anything like it. Little boats going up and down the river, and you go there to buy bananas and like that. You know I sent you that postcard? That was the day after the command performance. After we played, the king showed us the royal collection, and then he gave us each a present. Chinese jade, he said it was. I got a crazy pair of earrings, and there were cuff links for the boys. I don't know what happened to them. And I figured it would say in the newspaper stories how we had viewed the collection and what the presents were, so I wrote you that bit about selling my jewels. I guess it's good I did, huh?'

Our boat is caught in a current and spins madly around. Dhang paddles furiously. On the starboard side a huge log bobs in the water. We paddle over to it, and the log turns and begins swimming for us. It is a crocodile. We try to escape. It swims closer. *'How doth the little crocodile improve its shining tail,'* it says, *'and pour the waters of the Nile on every shining scale.'*

'We're on the Nile River,' Tuppence says. 'We're in Egypt, just in time for the ten plagues.' And then I was trying to mark the side of the house—the boat had turned into a house—with the blood of the paschal lamb, so that the angel of death would pass over the house, but it was raining endlessly, and the blood kept washing away, and the angel of death swept down and carried off Todor, and Annalya began to weep and wail.

Then Annalya spoke, but it wasn't Annalya, it was Tuppence again. 'I couldn't get what it was all about,' she was saying. 'They came into the hotel in the middle of the night and chloroformed us. I guess they had already stolen the jewels. The next thing I knew we were on our way up through Thailand and into Laos. They didn't feed us anything but rice, and anybody who asked questions got hit. And nobody understood a damn word they were saying. But I got some of the drift of what was happening or at least I think I did. They're

Laotian Communists, they're hooked up with something called the Pathet Lao, or maybe that's somebody's name. The bit was that they were going to make it look as though the five of us stole the jewels from the king and took them to Laos, the part of the country that's not run by the Communists. And then when we came north, they snatched us and executed us and returned the jewels. They were going to make the United States look bad and they were going to make the other government of Laos look bad, and it was supposed to do a lot of good for them and for the guerrillas in Thailand. Or something like that. And then they went and executed Kendall and Chick and Niles and Jimmie, just chopped their heads off one after the other. I thought they would do me, too, and maybe they would have or maybe not. I don't know. There was some kind of a snag on account of my being Kenyan, and maybe it would have screwed up their relations with Africa or some such. Or else that fat little mother just didn't want to deprive himself of the pleasure of balling me every day on his goddamned floor.'

'I was beautiful, and soft and warm and sweetly formed, with golden skin and long black hair,' said Tuppence, who had suddenly turned Oriental. 'And I wanted Dhang and would have gone with him, and just as he was on the point of making a woman of me . . .'

'Just as I was on the point of taking her,'

Dhang said, 'just then her father came into the room, and furious he was, and they put me in that room and beat the soles of my feet with long strips torn from old auto tires, and hung me up so that I had to stand on the tips of my toes, and told me they would cut off my purick, and swore they would cut off my head as well. I did not try to rape her, for she wanted me as I wanted her, and I would have been tender with her—'

'Evan, baby, I get the feeling that Dhang here is up tight sexually. You tell him to forget it, dig? He's a sweet little cat and all, but if you could tell him that this is just not my scene—'

'Heaven, friend, the black woman is your woman, yes? You said that you would get a woman for me, Yevan. I feel myself tortured and torn apart by demons. I will not touch the black woman, Evan, but I ache with desire and yearning. Yevan . . .'

The old man was riding on water skis pulled by a blazing bullock. Fire danced in his hair. He sang the 'Marseillaise' at the top of his voice and poured kerosene over himself and burned without being consumed. Then the bullock veered sharply to its right, and the burning old man bore down upon us, capsizing our boat, and the entire river turned into a sheet of icy flame.

'You should never have run away from us,' Barclay Houghton Hewlitt whispered in my ear. 'Don't you ever go down to the end of the

178

town unless you go down with me.' I looked at him, and he turned into Abel Vaudois. 'A good idea,' he said sagely. 'To grow opium poppies in the Jura, separate it from Switzerland, and sell the poppies to American veterans for Memorial Day. Is this not a typical American breakfast?' I agreed that it was, and he grinned like the Cheshire cat and turned into the Chief. 'That's a good cover story,' he said, 'but you'll need a cover story for it and then another cover story for that cover story, and we'll put them all together and bind them as a book and put your name on the cover. Now wait a moment,' he said, and he stepped around the corner and locked the dugout in the men's room of Kennedy Airport. I grabbed the locked door and began banging furiously on it, but it wouldn't open. I drew my pistol and shot at the lock, and the bullets bounced off and released clouds of cyanide gas, and I breathed it in and gasped, and the men's room taxied down the runway and was airborne, and we soared high over the blue Pacific until a divine hand reached out to snare us with a butterfly net and drag us down, down, down into an ocean of inky blackness.

*   *   *

'I think he's coming out of it,' a soft voice said. 'Him come out of big sleep. Oh, the hell with it.'

179

I opened my eyes. Tuppence was leaning solicitously over me; Dhang was looking over her shoulder. We seemed to be on dry land. I started to sit up, but they both reached to push me back down and told me to save my strength.

'I'm all right,' I said. And I was. The fever was gone now. I groped for memory and couldn't get the handle of it. I did not know where we were or how we had gotten there.

'What happened?'

'We almost lost you,' Tuppence said. 'Baby, you were in very bad shape. Feverish, and seeing things that weren't there, and talking to people who weren't around. All kinds of crazy languages. Dhang couldn't understand you, and neither could I. And Dhang and I couldn't understand each other, either, which made things like interesting. I tried to teach him a little English, but it didn't take very well. The only words he knows are the kind that get you thrown out of places. Did you teach him?'

'I guess so. Tuppence—'

'You hungry, baby? There's some fish baking. Dhang's pretty cute at catching fish. I guess it'll be done in a minute. He's got this way of cooking it, you dig a hole and build the fire on top of the fish, and you have them all wrapped up in leaves—'

'I know. It's his one recipe.' I sat up and looked around at the two of them and the fire and, a few yards off to the side, the river. Our

180

boat was beached on the bank.

'How long was I like that? A couple of hours?'

'Oh, wow.'

'What's the matter?'

'Would you believe three days, baby?'

'Frankly, no. Was I—'

'Three days. If we cut out of Tao Dan on Monday, then this is Thursday afternoon. Except that I sort of lost track of the days in Tao Dan, so it could be anything. But it's been three days. We just went on floating down the river all the time. Dhang kept turning up with things to eat, and we got a little water into you now and then but no food. Feed a cold and starve a fever, or is it the other way around? But whatever it was, you were in no kind of condition to eat anything.'

'How did you and Dhang manage?'

'Sign language, mostly. Tell you the truth, I was pretty useless most of the time. I did a little paddling, but he took care of the hard part, like pulling up on shore for the night and making the fires and scaring up something to eat. We took turns staying up with you. You don't remember any of it?'

'Bits and pieces.' I drew a breath. I was suddenly ravenous and I turned to Dhang, who had been maintaining a respectful silence. 'About that fish,' I said in Khmer.

'It will be ready soon, Heaven.'

'Good.'

'Your soul left your body and soared through the open reaches of the universe, Evan. But the woman and I waited for your soul to return, and from time to time it came back. The woman is good. She washed your head with water and helped me with your hair.'

'My hair?'

He lowered his eyes. 'It is gone, Evan.'

I put my hand on the top of my head. Nothing—I was as bald as a newly laid egg. I looked at Tuppence, who was trying bravely not to giggle. I said, 'What the hell?'

'It fell out in handfuls,' she said. 'Must have been the fever. You looked pretty patchy there for a while. You would lose some here and some there, you know, and you got to be something of a sight.'

'I can imagine.' I ran my hands over my bald dome. 'Dhang said you helped him with my hair. What's he talking about?'

'I'm not sure myself. We both gathered up all the hair as soon as it fell out, and at night we burned it in the fire. Very bloody tribal.'

'What for?'

'I don't know. He was very tense about it, and I figured like maybe he knew something.'

I asked Dhang. It seemed to have some deep religious significance, but either he couldn't explain it or I couldn't follow him. He seemed to feel that I owed my recovery at least in part to the ordeal by fire through which my

182

hair had passed. For all I knew, he was right, so I didn't argue.

'It's just as well,' I said. 'My hair never did look very Oriental. I must look pretty unusual.'

'When Yul Brynner does it, it looks pretty sexy.'

'I suppose it'll grow back in eventually. Do I look as sexy as Yul Brynner?'

She raised her eyebrows. 'You better look in the mirror.'

'What mirror?'

'You know—the river.'

I got unsteadily to my feet. I was very dizzy at first, but this passed quickly. I crossed the few yards to the river bank, dropped to my knees, and looked at my reflection.

It was shocking. I had lost an incredible amount of weight, and my skin was stretched tight over my bones. My skin did not need the tobacco juice treatment any more. I had turned a uniform yellowish hue all over. All of this combined with the utterly bald head left me looking not at all like myself. I had changed to fit my environment, all right. I looked more at home in an Indo-chinese jungle than I would have looked in Manhattan.

'Not exactly sexy,' I said.

'Not quite,' Tuppence agreed.

'I guess I can stand it if you can. Does anybody have any idea where we are?'

'Yes.'

'Where?'

183

'Lost.'

'Is that the best you can do?'

'We're on a river in the middle of a jungle,' Tuppence said. 'When you've seen one river, you've seen them all, and that goes for jungles as well. We've been paddling downstream, but I don't know how far. I suppose if you follow a river long enough, you get to an ocean. I'm not exactly Sheena, Queen of the Jungle, but I seem to remember that that's the general bag rivers are in, they flow into oceans.'

'It's a good general rule.'

'I'd love to be more specific—'

'I wouldn't mind it myself.'

'Anyway,' she said, 'the fish is ready. I suppose a person could get sick to death of fish, sooner or later. And more sooner than later. Let's eat, Bwana.'

I had two fishes and could have eaten more, but I was afraid of hitting my stomach with too much too soon. Dhang wanted to make camp for the night. I talked him out of it. He and Tuppence could sleep as safely in the boat as on dry land, and we would make much better time if we kept going through the night. I didn't mind paddling all night long. I felt it would be less nerve-wracking than sitting around listening to the jungle noises while the two of them slept.

We drowned the campfire, climbed into the boat, and pushed it back into the current. The river seemed wider than when we had started out, which rather stood to reason, since widening is a propensity of rivers, along with flowing into oceans. Tuppence sat in the stern this time, Dhang took up his post in the bow, and I was in the middle. This was ideal from a conversational standpoint; since I was the only one who could converse with both of the others, it was a logical spot for me.

First I talked with Dhang, who assured me he had kept his hands off my woman, although he admitted that the effort was becoming exceedingly difficult for him. He launched into an unembarrassed discussion of Tuppence's anatomical virtues and the uses to which various portions of her could be put, and I decided that it was just as well she couldn't understand a word he was saying.

Then I talked with Tuppence, and she went over the story of the capture and all the rest. It came through more or less as it had while I was delirious with fever but made a little more sense this time. Evidently the musicians were picked as pawns in a rather elaborate plot to discredit both the United States and the Souvanna Phouma neutralist regime in southern Laos. By returning the jewels and the heads of the Kendall Bayard Quartet, the Pathet Lao would show himself to be a staunch friend of Thailand and an implacable enemy of the thievery and deception that characterized U.S. imperialism. Now I could appreciate Tuppence's insistence upon recovering the jewels before we left the Tao Dan command post. If they stayed in Communist hands, the whole scheme could have been carried out more or less as planned.

But now, if our side returned the gems, the diplomatic tables would be turned. The Pathet Lao would get a black eye, American intelligence would come off looking good, State Department goodwill tours would not suffer a loss of prestige, and the Chief's faith in Evan Tanner would burn more brilliantly than ever. The CIA would retain its mandate to use Bangkok as a launching pad for Oriental fun and games, and the old Francophile in Tao Dan would not have died in vain.

I frankly wonder how much effect these little international ploys and counterploys have on the course of world events. Not very much, I suspect. Another report is filed in capitals throughout the world, another affair makes newspaper headlines for a day or three, and then the world returns to its usual routine of hypocrisy and intermittent violence. One throws a stone into a pool and attaches great significance to the manner in which ripple after ripple passes concentrically outward to the water's edge, but in truth once the ripples stop, the pool is as it was before, with the same water in it.

The Chief, I know, finds worlds of meaning in little gambits like this one. This only stands to reason—it is a rare man indeed who plays down the significance of his own life's work. Or perhaps, professional that he is, the Chief has outgrown the habit of looking at the greater implications of things. Perhaps instead he merely sees each little affair as an incident in an international game, worth a certain number of points on a worldwide scorecard, worth other points on another scorecard in which he is pitted against the CIA and military intelligence and the other game-playing agencies.

I decided that I did not too much care. I had come here because I thought Tuppence was in trouble, which turned out to be a massive understatement, and I had found and rescued Tuppence, and now we were on our way back to what we persist in calling civilization. If it made the Chief happy, that was an added bonus.

I just wanted to get home.

*   *   *

After the sun went down, there was a brief spell of rain. We got fairly well soaked, but it didn't last long enough to be really bad. Then the sky cleared, and there was enough of a moon to provide adequate visibility for nighttime paddling. Dhang paddled until he got tired. Then I took over. Tuppence stayed awake for a while before dozing off in the middle of a conversation. I kept paddling on through the night. The river was quite empty, the jungle alive with night sounds that I now found rather comforting. A jungle, I decided, was not quite so hostile a place as we are led to believe. I could understand now how people might choose to live their lives in it.

From time to time I pulled the paddle inside the boat and closed my eyes and rested. I felt completely recovered, and long before dawn I was hungry again. When the sky lightened, we beached the boat, and Dhang and I went out to look for food. I found some fruit that he told me was poisonous, and he brained a few lizards with the butt of his pistol and seemed surprised when Tuppence and I showed little enthusiasm for them. He managed to unearth some edible roots, and I picked some nonpoisonous berries. Tuppence and I made do with them. Dhang roasted the lizards and seemed to enjoy them considerably.

Around noon we stopped the boat again, and Dhang and I went exploring. We saw smoke rising off to our right and headed toward it, moving silently through the jungle. We had been a long time without seeing any other human beings. Where there is smoke there is also fire and often food, and living off the jungle can have its limitations.

We crept close to the campsite. Through a break in the undergrowth I saw uniformed men sitting around a campfire, talking and laughing. I listened closely but could not understand what they were saying. Whatever language they were speaking, it was not one I recognized. Dhang couldn't make it out either.

Some tribal dialect, I decided. I considered making ourselves known to them, then decided against it. If we didn't have a language in common with them, things could be extremely difficult. In all probability they were Laotian regulars, probably an antiguerrilla force. Dhang was still dressed in the uniform he had donned in Tao Dan, the uniform of a Pathet Laoist. If we couldn't tell them who we were, and if we couldn't be sure just who they were, things could get sticky. So we slipped away as silently as we had come, found Tuppence, got back into our dugout, and headed downstream once more.

And then, late in the afternoon, we heard a plane flying overhead. Dhang noticed it first. We heard the engines droning long before we caught sight of the craft and we craned our heads upward for a look at it, and the pilot came down for a look at us.

It was a jet fighter. I couldn't recognize the model but when it swooped downward, I made out U.S. Air Force insignia on the undersides of the swept-back wings.

'It's one of ours,' I said, and Tuppence and I began to wave furiously, and the plane continued its downward sweep.

And bullets plowed a furrow in the water

189

beside us.

'Evan! The mother's shooting at us!'

He missed us completely on that run. He came out of his dive, swung into a graceful turn, and headed our way again, machine guns open. The silly son of a bitch was trying to kill us.

'Overboard,' I shouted. 'Swim for shore! Fast!'

We leaped out of the dugout and into the water. Bullets riddled the water around us. I grabbed Tuppence and swam furiously for land. Dhang was off to the right, cutting the water with clean, brisk strokes. The pilot finished his run, made another illegal U-turn, and came back a third time.

We reached the bank, clambered ashore, dove into the cover of an overhang of vines and shrubs. The fighter let us alone and concentrated on the dugout. He made three more strafing runs at it and by now he was getting the hang of it. Bullets tore into the hollow wooden shell. By the end of the third run enough holes had been opened up, and the dugout had filled with water. It didn't exactly sink—it was, after all, wood—but its days of service were over. It was filled with water to the top. It was useless to us, and so were our guns.

The plane finished its third run, made another pass over the ship with the guns silent, evidently to assess the probable success of the mission. Then the pilot banked smartly, headed skyward, and flew away.

'Now he can go back to his base,' I said bitterly, 'and he can paint a dugout canoe on the side of the fuselage. The son of a bitch!'

'Baby, I don't get it. Why?'

'I don't know,' I said. 'Maybe—'

'Evan—the jewels!'

I swam back to the boat. The two leather bags of jewels were where we had left them, happily untouched by the bullets. But the boat was a lost cause entirely. I rescued the two jewel sacks and swam back to shore. A U.S. plane, I thought, disheartened. Just what we needed. With friends like him we didn't need enemies.

'Why did that mother shoot us up, Evan? And what do we do now?'

The second question was unanswerable. But I had the first one figured out and suddenly I knew where we were.

'Those soldiers we saw around noon were speaking Annamese,' I said. 'And they weren't Laotian regulars looking for guerrillas, but it still would have been a bad idea to join them.'

'Why?'

'Because we're in the middle of North Vietnam,' I said.

CHAPTER FOURTEEN

Dhang demanded a translation; once I had supplied it, he wanted an explanation. I told him the United States and North Vietnam were fighting, and that there were some guerrillas in South Vietnam called either the Vietcong or the National Liberation Front, depending who you listened to, who were fighting the government of South Vietnam. He asked how you could tell the North Vietnamese from the South Vietnamese, and I told him that you couldn't, but that it didn't really matter, because the leading strategists on both sides had evidently concluded that the only possible end to the confusion lay in killing everyone on both sides and everyone on neither side, as quickly as possible.

Then he asked another annoying question, one which Tuppence promptly echoed in English. 'What do we do now, Evan?'

I didn't answer either of them.

'We could surrender,' Tuppence suggested.

'To whom?'

'To the first people we meet. We're lost and we don't even have a goddamned boat. Suppose we just hit on the first cats we find and wave a white flag at them. What then?'

'They would take us to Hanoi and try us.'

'As what?'

192

'As war criminals. Or they might ship us back to the Pathet Lao. Or, most likely, they'd shoot us on the spot. I don't think the North Vietnamese Army is too keen on taking prisoners behind their own lines. They haven't had much experience at it except with captured pilots. With none of us speaking the language, they'd probably decide we weren't worth the trouble.' I shook my head wearily. 'Or else they'd figure out that we were part of an invading force operating in the north. Who knows? We might touch off an international incident. I wouldn't mind that so much, but I have the feeling we wouldn't survive the experience.'

'And don't forget the jewels.'

'I'd love to forget the jewels.'

'You haven't looked at them yet.'

'I don't particularly want to look at them. I should have left them in the river. Now we can't even chance surrendering to some peasants somewhere. They'd kill us for the jewels. You know, I'm not particularly ecstatic about our situation. I wish that goddamned river had led in some other direction.'

'How do we get out of North Vietnam?'

'I'm not all that certain that we do,' I said. 'But I guess the only way to do it is by going to South Vietnam. Which, logically enough, is south of North Vietnam.'

'So if we keep going south—'

'We get killed,' I finished for her.

193

'Oh.'

'But we have to try it. I think we can forget about the river. We could conceivably cut wood for a raft and lash it together with vines, but I'm not sure it would work. And the river seems a little too exposed. If that idiot was willing to waste a few hundred bullets on a dug-out canoe, he'd probably drop napalm on a raft.'

'If we don't use the river, what then?'

'Cut through the jungle,' I said. 'There's something called the Ho Chi Minh Trail— according to the newspapers, it's what the North Vietnamese soldiers use when they infiltrate into the south. I don't suppose there are any road signs on it, but if we head over that way, away from the river, we ought to hit some sort of route heading south. We'll have to travel by night, I'm afraid. We don't want to meet anyone at all because there's no one from here to the border we can count on as a friend. The local soldiers will be against us and so will the American planes. When they come over here, they shoot at anything that moves.'

'It doesn't sound so groovy suddenly.'

'It sounds terrible to me. Dhang's pretty good at jungles. If we follow his lead, we ought to do all right. We can sleep under cover during the day and move by night. I wish to hell we had the guns, or at least a couple of machetes. I've still got the dagger in my tunic, but I can't see us slaughtering much game with

194

it. Maybe we can pelt animals to death with the jewels.'

Tuppence looked closely at me. 'You sound a little hysterical,' she said. 'Is that fever coming back for a second round?'

'No,' I said. 'I'm just hysterical.'

*   *   *

By nightfall we had lost sight of the river without encountering a jungle trail heading south. We had huddled together twice while bands of natives, presumably civilians, passed within a few yards of us. And Tuppence and I had found out what lizard tastes like. I had figured it would taste like chicken, like all those other things that no one in his right mind would put in his stomach. It didn't. It tasted like salty rubber.

Walking cross-country in the darkness was about as much fun as stumbling up a downward-bound escalator. Dhang led the way, Tuppence followed, and I, loaded down with the two bags of jewels, brought up the rear. Tuppence kept falling down. If there was a root or vine anywhere in the neighborhood, she got a foot tangled in it and flopped on her face. After I picked her up for the twentieth time, I mentioned her great skill in jungle-jaunting.

'You ought to be better at this sort of thing,' I said. 'Think of the days of your youth, hunting Simba in the vast jungles of your native Kenya.'

'Shee,' she said, 'it. You ever been to Kenya, baby?'

'No.'

'Nairobi is like a modern city. No jungles. Sidewalks and everything. Everything's up to date in Nairobi.'

'Oh.'

'I would like to be there right now.'

'So would I,' I said, 'and I've never even been there.'

'How much of this jungle do you figure there is?'

'Miles and miles.'

'That pins it down.'

'Well, just figure that there's a lot of it.'

'There's already been a lot of it.' She fell down again, and I helped her to her feet.

We reached a southbound trail a few hours later. It was a path about four feet wide, and it couldn't have been the Ho Chi Minh Trail because it was far too narrow and overgrown to be used by a motorized column. I decided that this was just as well. We made much better time than we had when we were just stumbling blindly through the brush, but it was still very slow going. At this rate, I thought, we would spend months in the jungle. It would take us forever to reach the south.

We kept moving until daybreak. Dawn wasn't really that much of an event, for

196

relatively little light penetrated through the dense growth of vegetation overhead. There was a noticeable difference, though, enough to confirm my original idea that the daytime was a time for resting and hiding. We left the trail and made our way through the brush some thirty yards. Dhang and I cleared enough space for the three of us to stretch out. I think he found us something to eat, but I don't remember what it was. We were too exhausted to have any particular interest in food. It was simply fuel.

The trek had had one good effect. It had taken Dhang's mind off sex for the time being. He was too beat to think about it. As soon as he finished eating, he flopped in a heap to the ground, and within seconds his rhythmic breathing announced that he was asleep. Tuppence made a brief effort at conversation, then gave it up and curled up a few yards away. I stretched out and closed my eyes and waited for something to happen.

After about an hour I heard chanting off in the distance, and before long a band of foot soldiers went by along the trail. I didn't bother to see who they were or where they were going. I stayed silent and motionless, and Tuppence and Dhang went on sleeping.

Then, a while later, there was a series of explosions off to the north and east. Tuppence woke up almost at once and looked at me. 'Bombs,' I said.

'What the hell is that all about?'

'U.S. bombers striking at strategic targets in the north,' I intoned. 'Scratch a few more dugout canoes, I guess.'

'What happens if they drop bombs on us?'

'What do you suppose happens?'

'Uh-huh,' she said.

'A few months ago I signed a petition calling for a halt to the bombing in North Vietnam.'

'They should have listened to you, baby.'

'They didn't. Go back to sleep.'

She yawned. 'I can't.' She crawled over to me. 'Poor Evan,' she said softly. 'I got you in one sweet mess, didn't I?'

'Forget it.'

She touched my face. Her hand was cool in the heat of the jungle. 'You and Dhang could make out okay if I weren't around,' she said. 'You could hook up with those soldiers. The way you look now, no hair and that yellowy skin, you could pass.'

'Not without knowing the language.'

'You could fake it. But I'm afraid I'm just the wrong color.'

'You're also the wrong shape. But I wouldn't have you any other way.'

She kissed me. I took her in my arms, and she cuddled up against me. She had been through one hell of a lot without breaking down, and I wondered how much more she could take. It would be a long time before things got easier, if they did at all. She was

198

tough, hard, resilient, but everyone has a breaking point.

'Maybe we can find something to lighten your skin,' I said. 'Some native plants or something. Dhang might know.'

'If you do, just take the formula back to Harlem. You'll make a bloody fortune.'

She laughed softly. The bombs cracked again in the distance, but not so far in the distance as before. I tightened my arms around her and kissed her, and the noise of the bombing sounded a little less ominous.

And then, slowly, gently, both of us slightly embarrassed but driven past embarrassment by mutual need, we removed our clothes and found one another. She clutched me desperately, making urgent little sounds in the back of her throat. Her fingers stroked my bald head, moved down over my back. I kissed the richness of her dark brown breasts and stroked the black velvet skin on the insides of her thighs. She purred like a kitten and moaned like a freight train and sighed like a hiss of steam.

Until we had proved in the only truly effective way that we were both still alive. And, lying gently together, basking in the hazy yellow glow of life affirmed, once again becoming gradually aware of the bombs in the distance and the spiky jungle grass under our naked flesh, we opened our tired eyes and looked into the tormented eyes of Dhang.

'Oh,' Tuppence said.

Dhang turned away. Tuppence fumbled her way into her clothes. I put on my trousers and my tunic. Tuppence struggled to keep from laughing, and Dhang fought back tears.

And just when he had finally gotten his mind off sex, I thought. It hardly seemed fair.

CHAPTER FIFTEEN

Dhang was the first to hear them. He whirled sharply about, his hand cupped to his ear. I didn't hear anything. He dropped to the ground and pressed his ear against the trampled earth. It was the first time I had ever actually seen anyone with his ear to the ground. Any moment now, I thought, he would put his shoulder to the wheel and his nose to the grindstone.

I too dropped to the ground and pressed my ear against it. I could hear it then, the thud of vibrations. 'Sounds like a mechanized column,' I said. 'We'd better get out of the way.'

A few miles back our little trail had merged with a much wider path that also was heading southward. This new route was far more open, with patches of sky visible overhead. I hadn't been too enthusiastic over it at first. True, it proved we were on the right track, but new hazards presented themselves. It stood to reason that the route would see heavy North Vietnamese traffic, which meant we would have to be very careful if we wanted to remain undetected. Still more to the point, we were open to observation by U.S. planes and helicopters. The fact that they were on our side didn't do a hell of a lot of good unless they happened to realize it. It was bad enough in World War II, when American marines got shot up with hunks of the Sixth Avenue El. But at least those bullets were fired by the Japanese. It was even worse to get annihilated by one's own air force.

We were well hidden in the brush long before the advancing column came into sight. I rested the two sacks of jewels on the ground. A king's ransom, I thought, and much good they were doing us. They were an extraordinary collection; I had finally let avarice triumph over nonchalance a day earlier and had had a good look at them. Most were cut gems, diamonds and rubies and a preponderance of exceptional emeralds, along with a variety of stones I couldn't recognize. Many of them had started the trip in gleaming gold settings, but for expedience's sake the original thieves had pried them free and stowed them away in individual leather pouches. No doubt the gold had long since been melted down and disseminated through the Bangkok black market. It would have been enough to finance the operation for the Pathet Lao, and everything left over was gravy.

There were also some jade carvings, and I knew enough about jade to realize that they were exceptional. So we were toting a fortune, and it did us no more good than paper money or gold, neither of which would have been of any use. I would have traded the lot for a gun or a machete or a flashlight, anything that would have helped us cope with the jungle.

A horned beetle crawled from my foot to my leg. I flicked him away with my forefingers. Tuppence and Dhang crouched in silence on either side of me. The column of North Vietnamese was drawing close now. A trio of jeeps were in the lead, followed by a brace of motorized antiaircraft guns, a convoy of troop carriers, and, in the rear, four lumbering tanks.

And then, from the south, we heard the cheering sound of American air power.

Tuppence glanced at me, eyes wide with alarm, and I nodded. She pursed her lips and whistled soundlessly. Fly away, fellows, I urged them silently. Fly like birds. Don't be heroes today. Go bomb Hanoi or something. But don't drop anything around here.

They didn't listen to me.

Just a few yards from us the North Vietnamese braced themselves for action. The column ground to a halt, and the antiaircraft guns readied themselves for the encounter. The troop carriers peeled back their canvas tops and dozens of foot soldiers spilled out, rifles in hand. They scattered in the brush. We waited for them to stumble upon us, but almost all of them chose the other side of the road, and the ones who came over to our side were concentrated to the north of us.

The planes droned overhead. The tanks—Russian T-34's, the same sort I had seen in Korea—pointed their massive guns at the sky. Keep going, I urged the planes. Knock out the oil depots in Haiphong. Do anything, but go away.

In perfect formation the U.S. aircraft peeled off and dived for the trail. A pair of jet fighters led the way, flying directly into the stream of flak, peppering the trail with machine-gun shells. Behind them fighter bombers laid their eggs.

It was just what I thought it would be. Napalm.

The jungle burst into flame. 'Fall back,' I told Tuppence and Dhang. 'Don't even worry about the soldiers. They couldn't care less right now. Just get the hell out of the way of that fire.'

We scattered like field mice in a burning barn. More planes passed over the trail, and from the heart of the napalm fire came the report of high-impact shells. Now and then the anti-aircraft fire found its mark. One of the fighter-bombers took a blast in its middle and broke in half. A fighter evidently caught some flak in the cockpit, went out of control, and spiraled insanely off to the north, crashing and bursting at once into flame.

But the planes were giving better than they got. Three of the T-34's were out of action in no time at all, two taking direct hits, the third getting the backlash of the bomb that landed square atop the troop carrier in front of it. The ground troops screamed and died in the fire that raged around them.

We missed most of what happened, running crazily through the brush. We outran the napalm, then sprawled at last in a tangle of vines. And lay there, deafened by the sounds of battle, hearts shaken by the combined effect of exertion and panic, until the last burst of ground fire was still and the last plane flew south.

*   *   *

We had hated the jungle. Slogging through it, through the mud and the snakes and the insects and the treacherous vines, we had personified it and cursed it as an enemy. Now we crept toward the ruined army column and looked upon the alternative to the jungle. Acres of plant growth had been burned out of existence. What had been green was burned black, with little vestigial fires still raging at the perimeter. The air was filled with the scent of burning vegetation and the more pungent stench of roasted flesh. The wounded shrieked in agony or moaned in the throes of death. The dead were mercifully silent.

Those Vietnamese who remained unimpaired were unequal to the task of coping with the situation. We watched them from the sidelines, less afraid now of discovery. I scanned the row of ruined jeeps and antiaircraft guns and troop carriers and tanks.

'That's it,' I said.

'What?'

'Our passport. They got three of them, but one's still operable. All we have to do is get into it and roll.'

Tuppence looked at me as though I had gone over the edge. 'You rest a minute,' she said. 'The fever—'

'No fever. I'm talking about the tank.'

'Huh?'

I pointed. 'The T-thirty-four,' I said. 'The tank. That's our out. It doesn't matter what color you are inside one of those. We'll all be invisible. We can cut right through North Vietnam and across the demilitarized zone without anyone wondering who we are.'

'How do we get one?'

'Change places with the clowns inside it.'

'Suppose they don't go for the idea?'

'They're probably dead,' I said. 'They probably got cooked. If they don't come crawling out in the next few minutes, we can count on it. The napalm generates a hell of a lot of heat. But that last tank never took a

205

direct hit, and the machinery should be all right. Sooner or later it ought to cool off. By that time the rest of the column should be long gone.'

'Have you ever driven one of those things?'

'No.'

'Groovy.'

'I never paddled a dugout, either. Maybe I can figure it out.'

'You really think so?'

'Do you want to walk the rest of the way?'

'No.'

'Then it's worth a try.'

We waited on the sidelines while the uninjured soldiers and walking wounded rounded up as many of their wounded fellows as they could and made their way back north again. The air attack had been a fairly comprehensive success. What had begun as a motorized column left on foot, with all of their vehicles abandoned. Almost everything had been destroyed, and it was only barely possible that the one undamaged tank was still functional. But it seemed like a good gamble.

Around us the cries of the remaining wounded gradually faded. Some of them metamorphosed statistically from Wounded In Action to Killed In Action, dying quietly on either side of us. Others either passed out or gave up moaning when no one came to aid them. After a while I took a gun from a dead soldier, told the others to wait, and headed across the napalm-scorched clearing to the abandoned tank. From the ground a badly burned soldier called to me. There was nothing I could do for him. I went to the tank, and the metal hatch was still too hot to handle. The hatch was unfastened, which meant either that those inside had not bothered locking it, since after all they were not engaged with ground forces, or that they had escaped from the vehicle, or that they had died while trying to escape. I couldn't tell without opening the hatch. There was a general stench of burned flesh, but there was no way of knowing whether it came from within the tank or was merely part of the general aroma of roasted humanity that pervaded the entire region.

I went back to Tuppence and Dhang. It had been a while since our last meal but no one was very hungry. Tuppence was particularly shaken. Her eyes swept the battlefield, and she kept shaking her head. 'Why doesn't everybody leave everybody alone,' she said. 'I do not dig jungles. Remember how I told you they ought to take every jungle and rip it up and pave it with asphalt?' She had said this several times in the course of the journey. 'I'll take it all back now. Any jungle's better than this.'

'All the jungles will be gone soon.'

'Because of this? Bombs?'

'Not just that. Call it the advance of civilization. There's no room for jungles anymore. Too many people. There won't be any jungles or deserts left. We'll clear the jungles and irrigate the deserts, and I suppose someday we'll even level all the mountains, except for the ones we save for ski slopes. And instead of snakes and insects and animals and birds, there will be rows and rows of little square houses where there used to be jungles and deserts and mountains. And everyone will have enough to eat, and no one will die of sickening diseases, and everyone will speak Esperanto and have 2.7 children and pensions when they're old and nondenominational services when they die. And they'll all join bowling leagues and complain about crabgrass and watch color television, and when they talk to each other, Esperanto will be as good as anything else because they won't really have anything to say.'

'Evan—'

'Every town will have a park for the children to play in, and the park will have trees and shrubs for the people to look at. And the larger towns will have zoos so that the children can go to them and look at all the birds and animals that used to inhabit the earth. Everybody will buy frozen food at the supermarket and drink dietetic cola and get thirty-four percent fewer cavities and die of lung cancer. Everybody will be able to travel to far-off countries where everybody else lives in the same houses and goes to the same schools

208

and speaks the same language and eats the same food.' I looked at the scorched earth, and I turned around and looked at the wild green jungle. 'And it doesn't even matter who wins here,' I said, 'because either way it will turn out the same. If America wins, they'll pour in foreign aid until the whole country turns into one big Levittown. If the Communists win, they'll create the sort of worker's paradise you find all over Eastern Europe, with every house a perfect gray concrete block cube. It'll take them longer because they don't have as much money, but they'll make up for it by making it even uglier. There's a suburb of Cracow built since the war that looks as though it belongs on the outskirts of Cleveland. You can't blame it on any one nation. It's creeping monotony, it's the wave of the future.'

'There's a part of Nairobi that's getting like that.'

'Of course.'

'I think I'm getting hung up.'

'Look at the bright side,' I said. 'For all that's wrong with today's world, it's still better than tomorrow's.'

*   *   *

The next time I checked the tank, it was only slightly warm to the touch. I opened the hood and closed it again in a hurry. The tank had been carrying a full crew of three, and they

209

were still inside it but in far poorer condition than when they started out. I made Tuppence stay where she was while Dhang helped me empty the tank and disinfect it with petrol from one of the troop carriers. Then we both went into the jungle to vomit and returned to collect Tuppence and find out whether or not the tank still worked.

It was in surprisingly good shape, considering the condition of the crew. A triumph of modern warfare, I decided—one could destroy people without ruining valuable machinery. I played with the various gadgets inside the tank until I found the right combination to start it. The engine turned over but stalled dead after a few seconds. I guessed that it was out of fuel. Perhaps the heat had caused the fuel in the tank to vaporize, leaving a little in the carburetor to get it started. I'm not enough of a mechanic to know whether or not that's what happened, but Dhang and I collected fuel from two of the bombed-out tanks and put it into ours, and I started it up again, and it ran.

We climbed in, bringing along the jewels and a few guns salvaged from dead Vietnamese soldiers, including a sort of modified Sten gun. We also collected several cans of fuel that had been aboard one of the troop carriers. The Chinese writing on it meant nothing to me, so I didn't know whether one was supposed to run tanks on it or start

210

charcoal fires in a barbeque pit. I also didn't know how many miles a tank got on a gallon of fuel and hated the thought of running dry in the middle of the demilitarized zone.

We left the tank's hatch open to combat claustrophobia and asphyxiation, and we made ourselves as comfortable as possible. The control panel was in Russian, which helped. I settled myself behind it and felt like Bogart in *Sahara*. 'This baby'll start,' I said. 'All yuh gotta do is talk nice to her. We can beat the Krauts to the next water hole and hold 'em up till Waco gets back with help.' It wasn't a bad impression, but I could have saved my breath. Tuppence had never seen the movie, and Dhang, certain that I had just said something of monumental significance, insisted on a full literal translation and then asked what it meant. I told him to think about the women he would have when we reached Saigon. That set him off, and he spent the next ten minutes saying things Tuppence was lucky she couldn't understand.

The T-34 is a reasonably good tank. They gave us a hard time in Korea, and while I suppose they're considered obsolete now, this one wasn't so bad. The steering was simple and the ride, though uncomfortable, made up for it with the feeling of security it conveyed. I suddenly knew how a box turtle feels when he draws in his head and legs and closes the hinge on his plastron. All at once we didn't have to

211

worry about a thing. It didn't even matter if the locals became suspicious of us. We could ride right through them while the bullets bounced off us. No North Vietnamese soldier would be fool-hardy enough to fire a bazooka at one of his own tanks just because it seemed to be out of position. We had it made.

When we eventually overtook a long column of foot soldiers, the incredible value of our new vehicle made itself dramatically obvious. They must have heard us coming a long way off. By the time we were in sight of them, they had formed ranks on either side of the roadway to afford us easy passage. They took their caps off at our approach, and as we reached them a cheer went up all around us. They were glad to see us, they wanted to wish us all manner of luck on our way to meet the enemy. I fished around the control panel for a horn button to answer their salute. I guess tanks don't have horns, perhaps because they are not afraid of collisions. I gave up the hunt, took up a pistol, opened the hatch, and snapped off a volley of shots at the heavens. The soldiers roared their approval. After we had passed them, after they were out of sight, the sound of their hoarse applause still echoed around us.

'They really got excited,' Tuppence said.
'Yes.'
'They thought we were on their side.'
'Logical mistake.'

'I guess. Feels funny, doesn't it? All that cheering because they think we're out on our way to go shoot at *us*. Did you see their faces? Some of them are just kids.'

'Uh-huh. So are most of our Marines, and in a few days those kids you just saw will be lobbing mortar shells at them.'

'That's a bad scene.'

'That's war.'

'War,' she said, 'is hell.' I don't think she was quoting Sherman; I think the observation merely occurred to her, as it must to everyone, in every language.

I thought all the way back to Korea. The mud, bullets, the lousy rations, the bad summer, and worse winter. 'I wouldn't call it hell,' I said.

'No?'

'Not really. It's very alive and exciting, and it's fought by young men, and if they are young enough, they are convinced that what they are doing is very important. There's a hill, say, and the other side has the hill, and your side wants to take it, and you have to help your buddies and support them and you have to knock out the machine guns that are spraying bullets at you, and it's all very important, taking that hill. It's worth dying for.'

'All that for a hill.'

'You don't get the point. It doesn't really matter if it's a hill or a swamp or a plastic cesspool. It's something that seems very

213

important and worth dying for. If you have to die, you might as well go thinking you're doing it for a good reason. When you look at it that way, it doesn't matter if you die in combat or in your sleep, at eighteen or seventy-eight. Either way you wind up just as dead.

'But it only works when you're young. Because when you get older, you realize that there's nothing worth dying for, and that it doesn't matter very much whether you take a hill or not, because the world is full of hills, and you are the only you you've got.'

I thought of the old man in Tao Dan, riding his own funeral pyre into the mouth of hell for the glory of France. What, really, had he given his life for? For the safety of three strangers, none of whom was likely to do anything to enlarge the French colonial empire. For the glory of Charles de Gaulle, who would probably be at least as horrified as Ho Chi Minh himself at the thought of French reconquest of Indochina.

A wasted death? Hardly. He could have spent a few more years living on dead dreams and sucking marrow from the bones of memory. Instead he had died well, that old man.

I corrected myself. 'You don't have to be young,' I said. 'It's easier when you're young because then it comes naturally. You can still manage it when you're old, but then you have to talk yourself into it.'

I drove that tank all night. Tuppence and Dhang had dropped off to sleep muttering something about food and water, neither of which we had with us. We could get along without food, but water would become a problem before very long. I felt more and more like Bogart.

Somewhere between the middle of the night and dawn we lost the road. This could never have happened farther back, with the dense jungle on either side, but as we moved south the jungle gave way to vast stretches of open ground. I suppose we must have entered the demilitarized zone. I'm not too clear on the geography of the region, and even now I don't know exactly where we were. At any rate, I drove us right off the road without even noticing the difference. By the time I realized what had happened, there was no way to correct the error. The tank had a compass, so I kept us on a southerly course and hoped it would take us where we wanted to go. By the time the sky lightened, we were far out of sight of the road, so we kept on going south. When Tuppence woke up and asked where we were, I told her we were in Asia, and she told me nobody likes a smartass.

We were still in Asia when the plane attacked us.

We were still in the open, too, surrounded by vast reaches of grassland on either side. We were the only tank around, and he was the only plane, and unfortunately he was one of ours, and the tank was one of theirs. I didn't even see him until he started shooting at us. Then a rocket went off a few yards to our left, and we could feel the impact inside the tank.

'You idiot,' I screamed, 'we're on your side!'

'Maybe if you got out and waved to him—'

'I don't think so,' I said. I tracked him—he was banking now, preparing for another run. I looked at Dhang. It was too much for him, and he was cowering in one corner like a rat driven mad in an insoluble maze. The jungle was one thing, but riding in the belly of an iron monster while an iron bird shot at you, that was too much. He didn't want to have anything to do with it.

Neither did I. I had closed the hatch, of course, and now I watched the plane through the tank's sights. He was ready again. He came at us lower this time and fired off two rockets in turn. They were both wide on the left.

'He's a lousy shot,' I said. 'He's really terrible. We're barely a moving target, and he has all the room in the world to move around in. He should have blown us to hell by now.'

Tuppence was shaking.

'That's a small consolation,' I went on, 'but it's something. If all our fliers are this bad, it's amazing we're holding our own. Maybe he'll

216

run out of rockets.'

'Maybe we'll run out of tanks.'

He showed no sign of running out of rockets. His next pass brought him even lower, and I cooperated brilliantly by stalling the tank. This time he scored a near miss, and the tank rocked with the force of the explosion.

'He's getting warmer. Evan—'

'What?'

'Can't this thing shoot back?'

I looked up. There was a sort of steering wheel. I turned it, and our gun moved. There was a little door that you opened to insert a shell, and behind me on the floor there were shells. I snapped a command, and Dhang handed me a shell.

'They're probably duds,' I said. 'And I don't really know how to work this thing.'

'We have to do something.'

I loaded the shell, closed the little door, and searched the control panel for a gadget that would fire the thing. How the hell was I supposed to manipulate a tank gun to pick a plane out of the air? I had enough trouble manipulating a tank.

'Hey, wait a minute,' I said. 'I can't shoot him down.'

'What's wrong?'

'He's an American,' I said. 'That's one of our guys up there!'

'This is us down here,' Tuppence said.

He came on again, undaunted, diving

217

straight for us. I spun the little wheel and found the gun sights. I zeroed in on him as he swept down on us. He fired his rockets, and I fired the tank gun, and we rocked wildly with the force of all this explosive power, and he missed completely and so did we.

Dhang handed me another shell. 'I don't like this,' I said.

'Maybe you can just wing him, baby.'

'Sure.'

'Or maybe he'll give up and go home.'

I loaded the shell, put my eye to the sight, and started tracking him. I wondered if he were the same idiot who had put a few hundred holes in our poor little dugout. That one hadn't given up easily, either. At least now we could shoot back.

He began his run again, and I had the damnedest feeling that this was the last chance we were going to get. He was coming from our right front. I swung the gun at him and kept it on him, and I fired before he did.

'You hit him!'

The tail of the plane seemed to disintegrate. Then the plastic canopy popped open, and the pilot ejected, seat and all. He sailed high into the air, as if shot from a cannon. His parachute opened, and he floated gracefully down to earth.

I watched him land, roll, and come up on his feet. I felt a lot better then. It had been a kill or be killed situation, certainly, but that didn't change the fact that I had felt less than delighted at the thought of knocking American planes out of the sky. I started the engine, and the tank headed for him.

'He'll have flares,' I said. 'With any luck at all, somebody saw him go down. They'll send a helicopter for him, and we can hitch a ride on it.'

'He may not be happy to see us.'

'He'll be happy when he finds out we're us. Right now he's getting ready to surrender to a North Vietnamese tank.'

Except he wasn't. We had a good look at him as we drew closer. He was a very young Negro airman with a very valiant look on his face, and he had one hand on his hip while he used the other to point a pistol at our tank.

'I think he wants us to surrender,' I said. 'It's going to surprise the hell out of him when we do.'

We drew closer. I flipped open the hatch, and he sent a bullet whistling over the top of it.

'Cool it, soul brother,' Tuppence called out. 'The natives are friendly.'

CHAPTER SIXTEEN

In Saigon an Army doctor spent two hours checking me over. 'I think you're all right,' he said finally. He sounded vaguely disappointed. 'I can't find anything wrong with you. If I were you, I'd spend the next few weeks eating like a horse and sleeping like a bear. There's no trace of disease in your system. These tropical fevers are funny. We don't know as much about them as we'd like to. For instance, this one might recur. If it does, seek medical attention immediately.'

'I never would have thought of that.'

'Eh?'

'Nothing,' I said. 'What about my skin? I'm not usually this color.'

'A few days on a balanced diet should straighten you out.'

'And my hair?'

'You weren't bald before?'

'No.'

'Oh,' he said. 'Well, I suppose it will grow back in. Or possibly the loss will be permanent, it's hard to say. If it grows in, you have nothing to worry about. If, on the other hand, the hair loss does turn out to be permanent in nature, you have the choice of remaining bald or obtaining a hairpiece. Whichever you choose.'

'Thanks very much,' I said.

I got away from him and spent the next couple of hours with representatives of Army Intelligence and the CIA. They asked me a thousand questions ten times each. After it got boring, I said something about how hungry I was, and they sent someone out for sandwiches. It worked so well that I repeated this procedure every half hour or so, and every half hour they sent the kid running. I ate dozens of sandwiches and answered all their questions with my mouth full, and after a few hours of this in came Barclay Houghton Hewlitt.

It was Call-Me-Barclay in the flesh, and the flesh was as pink as ever. 'Tanner, old man,' he said, thrusting out a pink hand which I ignored. 'My God, you look dreadful, ha ha.'

'You look Caucasian,' I said. He blinked at me. I was true—after all that time in the jungle, after the constant company of Tuppence and Dhang and the occasional company of an infinity of Thais and Laos and Vietnamese, I felt that I had never in my life seen anything quite so Caucasian as Barclay Houghton Hewlitt.

I didn't explain it to him. I didn't even try.

He asked the same thousand questions that everyone else had asked, and I gave him the same answers. He was full of enthusiasm. He was full of plans. He was full of—

'This is more perfect than you can possibly realize,' he intoned. 'You and the girl will

221

return the jewels personally to His Majesty, of course. We'll arrange full press coverage. She's a colored gal, eh? That's a good angle, gives us a pitch that ought to appeal to the liberal press. Black and white together working to foil a Chicom plot. I think it would be good to draw the Chinese into it, ha ha. Black and white together. Won't hurt a bit, will it? Spike the rumors you hear about the Agency being prejudiced against the coons. You'd be amazed the rumors you hear, Tanner. Say, I got a look at that little jungle bunny. I think she'll photograph well, and that's a help.' He sort of winked at me. 'Bet she was hot as a pistol in the jungle, eh? Ha ha.'

'Ha ha.'

'Eh?'

'Ha ha, I said. The girl and I won't return the jewels personally to His Majesty.'

'But—'

'Say you recovered them yourself,' I suggested. 'Say it was an Agency operation all the way. If you want to juice it up, say that the Kendall Bayard Quartet was abducted because they attempted to prevent the robbery. You can play around with that if you want to, but the girl and I stay out of it. You blow my cover, and I'll blow your head off, ha ha.'

'Well, if that's the way you want it, Tanner—'

'That's exactly the way I want it.' I wasn't sure who outranked whom in this situation, but I felt that the best way to acquire power

222

was to act as if one already had it. 'Here are the jewels,' I said. 'Two sacks of them. You give them to the king and give him my love. Tell him Tuppence says he plays a very down clarinet, and Tuppence would know.'

He took the jewels, then hesitated. 'What about the gook you had with you? The Siamese kid? Want me to haul him back to Bangkok and give him the hero treatment?'

I had almost forgotten Dhang. 'No,' I said. 'Leave him out of it, too. His role is classified.' I thought for a moment. 'If you want a hero, I've got the man for you. An American airman named Marcus Garvey Cook.'

'What did he do?'

'At great personal risk he destroyed a pursuing North Vietnamese tank in the Demilitarized Zone. Then, disregarding his own safety, he crash-landed his plane in order to come to our rescue.' That was the story Airman Cook and I had dreamed up while waiting for a helicopter to find us. He hadn't wanted it known that he was capable of making that many runs at a tank without hitting it, and I wasn't thrilled at the idea of official records crediting me with the destruction of an American jet. So we knocked out the tank with a grenade in the gas tank and worked up a story for the folks at home. 'If you want a hero,' I said, 'he's your man.'

'I'll see what I can do.'

'What you can do in the meantime,' I said,

223

'is lend me a hundred dollars U.S.'

'I'm a little short—'

'Whatever you can spare, then.'

He gave me seventy dollars in crisp tens. 'And the Siamese kid?'

'I'll take care of him. I'm going to keep a promise.'

'Eh?'

'I'm giving him the hero treatment,' I said, 'right here in Saigon.'

*   *   *

The madam was a fat little Vietnamese with gold teeth and a permanent smile. Several soldiers had assured me her house was far and away the best in Saigon. The rooms were nicely appointed, the girls were clean and lovely, and the price was only ten dollars. She bowed us into the parlor and rang a little bell, and seven pretty things in slit skirts and high heels came tripping into the room and bowed before us.

Dhang was drooling, and his eyes were so bugged out that he looked like a frog. Maybe if one of them let him sleep on her pillow, he would turn into a prince.

He said, 'For me?'

'You're supposed to pick the one you want.'

'I want them all.'

'Well, pick the one you like best.'

'I like them all best. Purick in cunat . . .'

I counted the girls and recounted the money. Seven girls at ten dollars a girl was seventy dollars, which, providentially enough, was the sum Barclay Houghton Hewlitt had given me. That seemed too clear a sign from the gods to be ignored. But was it possible that little Dhang could possess seven women one after the other?

Anything was possible, I decided. Anything at all. With what Dhang had been through, it was conceivable that he had built up a stock of frustration that all the whores in Saigon couldn't cure. Anyway, he wanted all seven of them, and he deserved a shot at whatever he wanted. The son of a gun had paid his dues.

'He wants all seven of them,' I told the madam carefully. 'They are to go to him one at a time.' I gave her the money. 'Tell them to go in whatever order they wish. He loves them all.'

'He is Superman?'

'Perhaps.'

'Seven girls? Ho, boy!'

She relayed the instructions to the girls, who giggled and squealed at the prospect. I sat down, and one of the girls took Dhang in hand and led him away. The madam sat down beside me.

'And you, Joe? What you want?'

I thought it over. 'Do you have any betel nut?' I said finally. She frowned and said that she did not. 'In that case,' I said, 'what I'd really like is a nice cold glass of milk.'

*   *   *

He managed it. All seven of them, one right after the other, and when the last one went up to him, I began regretting that I hadn't saved a few dollars to bury him. But before long the girl came down, shaking her head in astonishment, and a few moments later down came Dhang. He was positively gorgeous in a Laotian Communist Army uniform. He swaggered like a drunken sailor and beamed like a lighthouse.

'I will never go back to Thailand,' he said. 'I will stay here in Saigon forever.'

'What will you do here?'

'Phuck,' he said succinctly.

'You'll need money,' I said. 'A lot of money, at this rate. What can you do?'

'Join the Army,' he said. 'Fight the V.C. Get good pay. Eat good food. And phuck.'

He sounded like a recruiting poster. He was sold on the idea, so I took him in tow and scouted around until I found a colonel who couldn't think of anyone else to shunt me off on. 'He'll be the best motivated soldier in the entire Army,' I told him. 'You couldn't ask for a more dedicated anti-Communist. He may be the only man who really knows what he's fighting for. He might win the war all by himself. Surely you can find a place for him.'

'I don't know,' the colonel said. 'You say he's Siamese?'

'That's right. Didn't Siam send troops?'

'A token unit. A hundred men, I think it was. Sure, that would be the place for him.' He shrugged. 'Hell of a note. Just five, six days ago a few of our planes got their signals crossed. You know how it is, this jungle and all. They hit the Thai volunteers with napalm and antipersonnel bombs, wiped the poor buggers out to the last man.'

'Oh.'

'One of those things, can't be helped, happens in every war.' It seemed to happen, I thought, with appalling frequency in this particular war. 'Goddamned shame you didn't show up a week or ten days earlier,' he went on. 'Could have put him in with those fellows easy as pie.'

'I'm glad we didn't.'

'Didn't what?'

'Show up on time for him to join them.'

'Oh? Why?'

'Because he'd be dead now,' I said.

'Oh,' the colonel said. 'Uh, yes, of course. Mmm. Hadn't thought of it that way, but you're right, aren't you? He'd be deader than hell by now, wouldn't he?'

I closed my eyes for a moment. Then I talked to him some more, and he wound up finding a way to have Dhang certified as an alien without his ever having set foot on U.S.

soil. They got around the requirement by having him stand on a flag in the American consulate. Then they let him enlist in the United States Army. Some genius wanted to send him stateside to Fort Dix for basic training, but we got it through to them that he was a combat veteran ready for assignment to the front lines. He wangled his first month's pay in advance and received instructions to report to his unit in three days. Then he and I said good-bye and shook hands solemnly, and away he went. I had a fair idea where he was going; I was only worried that his pay wouldn't last the three days.

*   *   *

That was about it. Tuppence and I caught a military flight to Tokyo and flew to San Francisco on Japan Air Lines, then hopped a Pan Am flight to New York. I ate about eight meals a day and decided that everyone looked hopelessly Caucasian, even in Japan. In New York Tuppence went straight to her agent's office to request a very safe and simple and square booking, and I took a cab to Kitty's place in Brooklyn and picked up Minna. She was crazy about the jade cat I had brought her, and Kitty went absolutely out of her mind when I gave her the emerald.

'It can't be real,' she said. 'When they're that size, they're never real.'

'It's real,' I told her. 'But don't wear it in Bangkok. It's hot.'

A few days later I peddled the three other emeralds I had taken. A jeweler on 47th Street gave me more than I had expected for them. I didn't think the king of Siam would miss a few stones; if he did, he could blame the Pathet Lao or the CIA, whichever he chose. And it was only sensible that I cover expenses. I had lost a load of cash at the guerrilla camp in Thailand and a flashlight battery full of gold in Tao Dan, not to mention all the pounds of me that had gone down the drain in the course of things. A couple of emeralds and a jade kitten seemed reasonable compensation.

Tuppence, for her part, had appropriated a ruby the size of a robin's egg, which she wore back to the States in her navel.

What else? The Chief saw me, summoning me to the meeting by having some kid pass a note to Minna. I didn't much care for that. It was bad enough that he bothered me all the time; I didn't want him involving the child. She handed the note on to me and told me, in Armenian, that all Turks are the swine-loving spawn of the devil. I told her not to believe everything that Kitty's grandmother told her, and then I went to meet the pudgy man from Washington.

'You continue to amaze me,' he said. 'Everybody goes on a mission equipped with a cover story, Tanner. It's standard procedure.

But only you could come out of a mission with still another cover story. You must have handled the opium job in nothing flat.'

'Oh,' I said. I had wholly forgotten that nonsense about the opium.

'We're starting to get word already. Whoever your connections are, they don't fool around, do they? Preliminary operations for the cultivation of opium are already underway in extensive stretches of Modonoland. I hadn't even heard of the damned country until this came up. It was part of either Nigeria or Tanzania until a couple of months ago, when it seceded. The growers have the full cooperation of the Modonoland government, and there's no reason why this shouldn't pull the rug out from under the Red Chinese opium trade.' He winked. 'Of course, we'd hate to be officially involved. Can't subsidize the opium trade with one hand and lock up a lot of poor little junkies with the other. That's why it's so perfect that you kept the whole thing under wraps with the cover story of the Siamese jewels.' He beamed. 'Everybody's happy about this one, Tanner. Right straight up to the top. I mean everybody.'

But everybody wasn't happy. I wasn't happy, for one. I went back to my apartment, and I looked at the heroin addicts in the streets, and I walked upstairs and sat down and wasn't happy at all. I tried telling myself it was a coincidence, and that lasted about three days.

Then a letter arrived with a Macao postmark, and inside it was a check for one hundred thousand Swiss francs drawn on the Bank Leu in Zurich. A note from Abel said, 'One good turn merits another. Autonomy for the Jura!'

So I had done the world a bad turn, and I had in return a piece of paper worth roughly twenty-three thousand American dollars. It bothered me for a long time. I didn't know what in hell to do with it. Finally I wound up donating half of it to Synanon—they've had exceptionally good results treating heroin addicts. And with the remainder I founded an organization aimed at over-throwing the government of Modonoland and burning the opium fields to the ground.

Chivers Large Print Direct

If you have enjoyed this Large Print book and would like to build up your own collection of Large Print books and have them delivered direct to your door, please contact **Chivers Large Print Direct**.

Chivers Large Print Direct offers you a full service:

★ **Created to support your local library**

★ **Delivery direct to your door**

★ **Easy-to-read type and attractively bound**

★ **The very best authors**

★ **Special low prices**

For further details either call Customer Services on 01225 443400 or write to us at

Chivers Large Print Direct
FREEPOST (BA 1686/1)
Bath
BA1 3QZ